WHAT A BITCH!

Chrystal Rose was born in Lagos, Nigeria, in 1962 and came to Britain when she was eleven months old. A single mother at seventeen, she has been a model, studied acting at the Royal Court Youth Theatre, worked as a clerk, journalist, radio broadcaster and now has her own weekly TV show on Carlton inspired by the Oprah Winfrey show.

What a Bitch!

CHRYSTAL ROSE

FOURTH ESTATE · *London*

First published in Great Britain in 1996 by
Fourth Estate Limited
6 Salem Road
London
W2 4BU

1 3 5 7 9 10 8 6 4 2

A catalogue record for this book is available from the
British Library

ISBN 1-85702-439-7

Typeset by Palimpsest Book Production Limited,
Polmont, Stirlingshire
Printed in Great Britain by
Clays Ltd, St Ives plc

This book is dedicated to all bitches, worldwide.
If not for you, I wouldn't have been inspired to write it.

Thanks to:

*Chi-chi, Sharon, Bernard and Shelley for taking the time
to read the first draft.*

Tony Fairweather.

Caroline Upcher for putting a light under my butt.

Jan Boxshall for being so efficient.

And my beautiful daughter, Louise.

Mum, Dad, Emma, Kemmy – respect.

Brixton, London, July 1985

The month of July had been filled with the hottest days and the warmest nights so far that year and the smell from overturned dustbins and the litter of discarded fast food and rotten vegetables from the market had attracted the rats. Everything about the area was gloomy. Even the parked cars scattered about the streets seemed to be tilting sideways down to the gutter. All the signs of a serious concrete jungle could not be camouflaged despite the new buildings in amongst the tattered-looking tower blocks. Many homes still housing tenants had broken or boarded-up windows. Only those who lived above the fifth floor out of reach of thrown missiles could look out through windows that were still intact.

And the noise never stopped: pop, soul and reggae blasting out from homes in every direction.

Except for one flat where the occupant was as oblivious to the music as the rats outside.

'What have you done? Hold on. Just wait there!'

He raced into the building leaving her leaning with her back against the car, holding her head. Her hands were covered in blood.

When he arrived at the flat he slowed down. He couldn't possibly have prepared himself for what he saw. The arms flopped loosely either side of the body sprawled on the floor. There seemed to be pieces missing from it.

And the blood was everywhere, on the carpets and splashed around the surrounding walls. On the floor lay a knife with a long blood-stained blade.

Did she realise what she had done? They were only supposed to be going out to dinner!

1

Ealing, London, 1962

He stood there, tall, suave and sophisticated. At five years old, Grace's only references for such a romantic hero were the images in the drama programmes she watched on the black and white television set sitting on the tall wooden cabinet in the corner of her parents' one-bedroomed flat, and the pictures of knights in shining armour who swept the heroines off their feet in her colourful bedtime story books.

Grace giggled. She was hiding behind the settee, peeping out to gaze in admiration at her uncle. What was it about him? He was everything and more. Good-looking, kind, and she knew that, even though each time he visited he had a different girl on his arm, one day when she was grown-up like her mum she was going to be his one and only Sleeping Beauty. He was just waiting for her to grow up before he could sweep her off her feet and carry her away into the sunset. She knew that he couldn't do it on horseback, like the heroes in her fairytale books, because people drove cars nowadays, but Grace didn't care. One day, Grace knew, she was definitely going to walk down the aisle with this man.

'Where's my favourite niece? Look, Grace. Look what I've got for you.' Kema pulled out a floppy cream-coloured doll from a white plastic bag. 'Chinella, where is she? I thought you said that she was off school with a cold today?'

Grace's mother walked into the room laden with folded laundry. 'Hi, Ola.' Chinella abruptly acknowledged Kema's latest fly-by-night. It was only about ten in the morning yet there was Ola standing right in front of her, seemingly eight foot tall, with legs that stretched for miles, barely covered by her brown rabbit-fur jacket. Chinella wondered whether she was wearing anything else under it.

She was typical of Kema's women. Kema was a playboy. OK, so he was single and had every right to have as many different women as he wanted, but Chinella wished he wouldn't keep bringing them around to her home, and certainly not first thing in the morning.

'She is. She's out the back, I think. So what brings you over to these parts so early in the morning? Oh, not another toy, Kema. You're spoiling her. And why did you get a doll that colour?'

'Goodness! Who got out of the wrong side of bed this morning, then? Just tell me if I'm not welcome and I'll go.' Chinella said nothing. Kema tried to make light of a bad start. 'Ola needed to meet someone who lives in this area and so I thought I could kill two birds with one stone, drop her down here and come and visit my best sister-in-law.'

'I'm your only sister-in-law!'

'That's beside the point. And by the way, all dolls are this colour.' He looked over at Ola for support.

But Chinella was not finished.

'Well it's not exactly representative of us, is it? Just

in case you hadn't noticed, we're black, not white. Why don't they make black dolls in this country?'

Kema was shocked at Chinella's reaction. 'Well . . . I . . . I didn't see any black dolls in the shop so I . . .'

'See now, that's the bloody problem with this country. They don't cater for any other race but their own. They invite us over and then act as though we're unwelcome aliens.'

Kema knew that when his sister-in-law launched into this particular argument it was best for him to remain silent and Ola realised now might be the time to make her excuses and leave. Once she had gone Kema asked Chinella gently, 'It's your landlord again, right?'

'What is?'

'Your mood.'

'No. I always talk like this.' Kema just stared at her, prompting her to admit, 'Well, who else? Yeah, it's the bloody landlord. He's got such a nerve.'

Now he had established Chinella's anger was not directed at him Kema relaxed and flopped down on the settee, draping his feet over the armrest unaware that Grace was curled up behind him, keeping very quiet and still.

'What's he done now?'

'You mean what hasn't he done? In fact, what else is there *left* for him to do after everything else, putting the rent up four times in the last year, not fixing the ceiling for three weeks after it collapsed, leaving the old furniture from the upstairs flat obstructing the passageway for the last six months – where's Grace supposed to play with her friends? I mean, need I go on?'

'Well, what's he done this time?'

'He says . . . he says that we've got to move out and he's given us two weeks' notice.'

'Why? When did he say that?'

Chinella looked down at the pronounced bulge in front of her. She could no longer hide the fact that baby number two was on its way. Their landlord had been looking for any excuse to get rid of them since the time her husband, Falmi, had nearly punched his lights out last year, slamming him up against the wall after the landlord had patronisingly patted Chinella's bottom. Since then he'd obviously decided that they had to go, and now he had the perfect excuse. On her way back from taking Grace to the doctors that morning he had cornered her and told her of his decision, which was final. There was no way that his one-bedroom flat could house two adults and two children, no way.

'So move then,' Kema told her without reservation. 'I don't understand why you haven't moved before. Falmi's forever working. You're not short of money. Why is it that you want to stay in this place anyway? You can live anywhere in London. It doesn't have to be Ealing.'

'You know why I want to stay here; I've told you before. All of my friends are here. We came over from Nigeria together and I want to stay near them.'

'But that was five years ago and anyway, it doesn't mean that you have to stay put in this particular flat in Ealing in order to see your friends, does it? Find another flat to rent in the area. I can't understand what the problem is.'

'That's because you haven't got any children yet, well, none that you know about anyway. You're not married, you're a free agent and landlords don't see you as undesirable the way they do us. And we've another baby on the way. Not that it would matter if we were white. Oh, I shouldn't have to explain this to you.'

'I do understand, you know. I do. Heaven knows it wasn't easy for me either, but that's why I decided to live where I do. I don't get any hassle at all, at least not until I leave the area.' Kema glanced at Chinella who looked unswayed. 'OK, so why don't you get on the property ladder? Buy a house, then. Weren't you looking into that before?'

'Yeah, but there are so many obstacles even in getting a mortgage. And how are we supposed to get things together in two weeks? Besides, we really have been through everything and renting is best for us at the moment. We just have to sort ourselves out, and fast.'

'My advice is the same as it's always been,' said Kema. 'Move. Ealing isn't really a black area anyway. If you move to an area where there are a lot of black people, you won't come up against half the problems that you're encountering now.'

'You might well be right, but then we're going to have to make so many adjustments . . . so many changes.'

'So what are you saying? That you're scared of change? That you'd rather keep fighting for this place, which is too small, than look into moving because it will mean making some changes? And what's best? Living in an area where you're not wanted and where you're not happy, or moving to an area and making a few changes that will give you all a better start in life? Think about it. It makes so much sense.'

Chinella remained silent for a while as she joined Kema on the settee. She put down the laundry and gently rubbed her stomach.

'It would be a solution. Look how often I've moved. It's no big deal.' Kema continued his argument.

'Yes, but that's because you're trying to hide from husbands who've found out that you're having an affair with their wives, or girlfriends who have found out that you were two-timing them.'

'Yes, well, we'll say no more about that, just come to Brixton,' Kema persisted. 'You'd be right on my doorstep and . . . I could visit you daily then.'

'D'you know what, you nearly had me convinced until you added that bit.'

'Very funny.'

'No, seriously. I might as well mention this now because

7

it has been bothering me. You keep bringing different women around here. Every time you come, practically, it's someone new. I don't think it's good for Grace to see you with so many different women.'

'What's Grace got to do with anything?'

'Well, you're setting her a bad example.'

'Don't be silly.'

'She idolises you. And she must have noticed that every single time you come, you're with someone new.'

'Chinella. Stop exaggerating. I've been with Ola for . . .'

'Two weeks! Now that's a record.'

'Look, this hasn't got anything to do with Grace. If you don't want me to bring my girlfriends round to meet you, I won't. You keep saying to treat your home as though it was mine, but then when I do . . .'

'Come on, Kema. I'm talking about respect. Of course I want to meet your girlfriend, but maybe when you're having a serious relationship, not just every chick that you pick up. Anyway, aren't you getting on a bit now? You're what, thirty-eight? You really should be thinking about settling down, you know?'

'Umm, maybe, but that's a conversation for us to have some other time. You know my intention isn't to stay here for long. I'm just enjoying myself while I'm here, having a good time, but I hear what you say and I will respect your wishes. I won't bring any more women around, OK? Now, getting back to your problem . . .'

'Yeah, we did drift a bit. Well, OK. I think that you might be right, Kema. A move is as good as a change. Huh!' Chinella added with a sigh.

'What?'

'I wonder how Falmi will react to this when he comes home from work. He'll definitely want to have a word with the landlord. But that really isn't the right course of action. We've got a lot to talk about. There's just so much to do in so little time.'

'Well why don't we make a start now, today? What were you going to do today anyway? I've got the day off so I can drive you to Brixton and we can go and see some of the estate agents in the area.'

'Oh, Kema. You're so persuasive.'

'There's nothing persuasive in what I've been saying. It's just common sense. You've only got two weeks, why waste another day?'

'Right, right. OK. Let me just get myself together, and Grace, and then we're all yours . . . and Kema?'

'What?'

'Thanks.'

'I haven't done anything.'

'You've put all of my problems into perspective. So . . . thanks.'

Chinella thought about the regrets she had mentioned to Kema and wondered what Falmi's greatest concern would be. She thought about Grace's friends at school. If they moved out of Ealing Grace would have to go to a new school. Grace loved school and did exceptionally well. She would always have her parents' support, but Chinella knew it was equally important for Grace to understand as early as possible the value of education. Grace had listened to and welcomed endless encouraging remarks from her father. Both he and Chinella were well aware of Grace's intelligence and both spoke about the opportunities open to people who took full advantage of the British educational system.

Falmi was particularly keen that Grace should make full use of her education. He worked on a production line at the Wall's factory in Acton. He was capable of much more but didn't have the qualifications on paper to prove it.

Over and over he told Grace:

'Having the brain power is not enough. Your academic grades are all important. Education is a chance for you to have countless advantages in later life and a chance to be the best on every conceivable level. It might be your only route to success.'

Chinella knew that Falmi's greatest concern would be about finding the best school for Grace to attend if they moved. Then she began to fret about Grace's reaction. But she needn't have worried.

Curled up behind the settee, Grace was happy. She was so pleased with everything that she had overheard. She especially liked the idea that her uncle could no longer bring other ladies to the flat, and wasn't it just like her beautiful hero to have found the solution to all the family's problems? Now she was going to be living in the same area as the man she was going to marry. Grace chuckled to herself.

Already, at just five, Grace had an enquiring mind which could absorb a mass of information. Out of boredom, out of a need to be constantly stretched, she had unconsciously developed a liking for using her extraordinary mental prowess to exert power over other children, children she knew to be weaker than herself. She no longer found satisfaction just from getting the highest marks in spelling tests. That came too easily. She found that she got a lot more out of wreaking havoc on less capable pupils and then sitting back and watching them suffer the consequences of her actions.

One day she put half of some worms that she had gathered over a weekend into her teacher's handbag at break time. Later that day the other half was found in Eddy Fisher's desk, along with some plastic coins which were used to teach the children to count money. Grace had stolen them from the classroom cupboard because she discovered she could use them in place of real coins to obtain bubble gum from the school machine. But one of the plastic coins had got stuck in the machine and was bound to be discovered. Immediately she saw another way to incriminate poor Eddy Fisher and slipped some plastic coins into his desk. The headmaster brought it up in assembly, saying that all plastic coins were school property and the use of them in any way, other than in lessons, was against the law. No other child in the assembly hall knew what he was talking about, but Grace did. She knew that Eddy Fisher was going to get into big trouble when she saw his mum and dad go into the head's office the next day. But what did she care? She was too busy setting someone else up for a fall.

It was easy for her to get children into trouble and the more she did it, the more she enjoyed it. What else was there for a clever girl like her to do when the teachers at the school couldn't see the wood for the trees? She was never caught and so something that started out of boredom was unfolding into the covert behaviour of a young delinquent. But she justified it by telling herself that she was only putting her father's words into action. People, he had said, had to be aware of her mind and how much could be done with it. It became her mission to toy with a system that didn't cater for children of her capabilities. So there was nothing much to be missed at school if they moved, and in terms of what she was going to gain there was absolutely no contest.

'Grace!' she heard her mother bellow. 'Get your coat, we're going out.' Grace crawled on her hands and knees out of the room and then sprang to her feet. Unlike most occasions, she didn't need to be told twice.

'That was quick,' Kema laughed as Grace rushed in and stood before the man she firmly believed would be her future husband, her coat bundled under her arm. He reached into his jacket pocket and took out a handkerchief which he used to wipe Grace's nose made red from her cold.

'Look how pretty you are under there,' he told her kindly, without really looking at her.

Grace was thrilled. He thought she was beautiful! She knew it! She knew from as far back as she could remember that this was the man for her, and now she knew for certain; it had all been confirmed. It wasn't one-sided at all, he felt exactly the same as she did, but, oh dear, they would still have to wait until she was Mum's age, until she had grown into a woman. Grace was so excited at Kema's confession that she didn't hear him ask her to lift up her arm as he tried to guide it into the sleeve of her coat. She might be a scheming little trickster at school but, in her misguided love for her uncle, Grace was still an innocent child.

Grace was used to trips out with her mother and Kema. With her father working Monday to Saturday, Chinella and Grace spent a lot of time together. If it was a nice day, they'd go for a stroll through the park after school and play on the roundabouts and slides and Chinella used to push her on the swings, until her pregnancy became so advanced that her doctor told her she shouldn't put a lot of strain on her back. Apparently there'd been some complications when Grace was born and she had been delivered two months prematurely: Chinella had to be extra careful through this pregnancy.

Grace was encouraged to be a part of the whole pregnancy period. She was told about all the changes that Chinella was going through and felt her mother's lump, as she called it, as it grew. But the impending arrival didn't only affect her mother. There would be one major difference in Grace's own life. She would no longer be her parent's only consideration and, quite frankly, she wasn't terribly pleased about that. For so long it had been Grace this and Grace that. She was the one they talked about. She was called her uncle's favourite niece. What higher accolade could there be? She was special, but now, now there was a shift in emphasis. Grace's feelings seemed to be a secondary consideration and hey, wasn't this all down to the imminent arrival of a new baby boy?

Grace had decided that her mother was having a boy. That's what she'd heard her dad say and, anyway, they already had a girl. Another would be one too many and would only get in the way. Mind you, who really cared what her mother was having? It meant they were going to have to move, didn't it? And that meant that she would be near her uncle.

As far back as Grace could remember, Saturdays were spent shopping for food and other stuff and Chinella had it down to a fine art. They always held hands as they shopped and, until recently, they had a workable system. First they'd go to the Co-op on the High Street to buy mostly tinned and packaged foods, then they'd take the 207 bus down to the market in Shepherd's Bush and buy vegetables, fish and meat. Saturday lunchtime was spent in a café where they had sandwiches and a cream cake and then they'd go off to buy anything else that was needed, like clothes and household items.

But now even that routine had changed. The doctor had advised Chinella not to carry heavy bags any more and, although Grace was strong and very big for her age, she couldn't carry everything. Falmi was going to give up his Saturday shift so he could do all of the shopping, but then Kema had volunteered to help out and for the last eight weeks had picked them up every Saturday.

But today was a Thursday. Today was special. Today her uncle had as good as proposed to her.

The fifth flat they went to see that day seemed ideal. Chinella told Grace, 'You can have your own room. This one could be yours, you'd like that, wouldn't you? Are you listening to me?' But Grace was too busy watching her uncle try to tune in the radio that had been abandoned by the previous tenants.

'OK, so you like the flat?' asked Kema.

'Sure, it's great,' Chinella agreed. Grace sat on the carpet swinging her new doll by its plaited hair. This man knew everything. He was just like Prince Charming in her books. And now she had a prince all to herself.

Falmi received the news of their forthcoming eviction more graciously than Chinella had expected. He felt better for knowing that he owed four weeks' rent. That debt had come about simply because the landlord hadn't been round to collect it of late. There was no way he was going to get the money now.

Moving also meant changing the hospital in which his second child was going to be delivered, but even before finalising those details Falmi phoned Brixton Town Hall's Education Department to get a list of the schools which Grace could attend. He took time off and visited a few: it was so important to get the very best of what was available for her. He talked to Grace about the prospect of moving to a new school, to make sure she was prepared to deal with a different environment and a new teacher.

They moved into Flat One, Carlton Court, Brixton Lane, London SW9 two weeks later. Their weekly shopping trips with Kema increased to twice and three times weekly as the birth drew nearer but the difference was that, every time something was bought, it wasn't bought for Grace but for the unborn child.

Finally Chinella went into hospital.

'What's his name?' Grace assumed that the doctor approaching her father was about to tell them some good news.

'It's not a boy. Mr Ideh? Congratulations! You have a very healthy baby girl.'

From that day on, nothing was the same. Grace was no longer the priority. Now there was Tiffany Ideh. Tiffany Ideh? What a silly name they had given her baby sister.

And yet – what did she care? Life was still fine. She still saw Uncle Kema daily so she was happy, wasn't she?

Or happy-ish.

2

Brixton, 1966

'Mummy! Mummy! Grace just hit me again,' Tiffany bawled for the umpteenth time. The fear in her eyes reflected Grace's ice-cold glare.

There was so much that Grace wanted to say and do to her little sister, but as usual there was no time. The sound of their mother's footsteps could be heard approaching.

Even though Chinella was on her way to the rescue, Tiffany retreated a few steps in terror. This wasn't the first time she had had to endure such an unwarranted attack. It seemed she had been on the receiving end of Grace's hostility a thousand times before. But why? Why was Grace always doing this to her? What had she done to Grace today? She hadn't been in her room. She hadn't messed with any of her toys. Mummy had just bought her a new doll when they were out shopping, the one that Grace had wrenched out of her hand and thrown on to the floor before she took Tiffany's skin between her fingers and pinched it. And that had really hurt. As Tiffany looked down at her arm she could see the area was red and swollen. It wasn't fair. She definitely hadn't done anything this time.

Chinella swept up her youngest daughter and immediately saw the swelling. She sighed. There was no point in trying to get an explanation out of Grace as to what had happened. For about a year these attacks had become an all too regular occurrence and there was never any real justification for them. Had it really got to the stage where she not only had to take Tiffany shopping with her all the time, but she couldn't even leave her alone in the same room as Grace?

'You're the eldest, Grace.' She said sternly. 'You're supposed to be helping me with your younger sister, not terrorising her.'

Chinella waited for a sign of remorse, an apology – anything – but Grace remained silent and stared at her mother, who was cuddling what she saw as the enemy. How could such a small person cause so many problems? What was it about Tiffany that made her always grab all the attention? What about her, Grace? For instance, what had her mother brought her back from shopping? Nothing . . . again. Wasn't she as important as Tiffany? Why didn't her mother ever take her shopping any more? She had promised not to snatch money out of the till again, and she had only done that because the cashier had been talking about how pretty Tiffany was instead of giving Mum her change. She had only done it to divert attention. She wasn't a thief. So why had she been demoted to just a babysitter? 'Look after Tiffany, Grace. Make sure that the pots aren't boiling over, Grace. Go and get a spoon for Tiffany, Grace. Go, go, go, go, go.' It seemed that, other than fetching and carrying for her parents and Tiffany, she had no use. Didn't they realise how much she needed to be cared for and loved, just like it used to be before brat-face came along? Brat-face? A stupid name which nobody else but Grace would use, as Tiffany's face looked anything but brattish.

Even at the tender age of four Tiffany was beautiful,

beautiful in an angelic way which *everybody* noticed and *everybody* commented on. And *that* was the major stumbling block for Grace; the reason why, a year ago, she had begun to turn into a monster. She would always remember the day that Tiffany had forced the real Grace out into the spotlight. On that day she'd been writing in her exercise book, doing some of the sums that she had asked her mother to set her, when Uncle Kema walked in. He had walked over to her and asked what she was up to. She explained and he glanced at the book and patted her on the head. And that was it. No words of praise for her hard work. No comments about how pretty she was. Instead her beloved Uncle Kema had turned his attention to Tiffany, who was sitting quietly in the corner with a colouring book and packets of felt-tip pens. He snuggled down beside her and started to help her colour in the multi-coloured elephant. Grace had watched in mounting horror. What was he doing spending that amount of time with her sister? She noticed her uncle kept staring at Tiffany.

'Do you like colouring, Tiffany?' he had asked.

'Yes.'

'Hey, have you started to think about what you want to be when you grow up?'

'No.'

'Well, you're pretty good at colouring. You're staying well within those lines, aren't you?'

'Yes.'

'And the colours that you're using are great.'

Tiffany just giggled, which helped to emphasise her two cute dimples.

'Maybe you're going to be an artist, or something. What d'you think?' And as Grace watched, Kema raised Tiffany in the air and bounced her up and down. Tiffany was having so much fun. Grace closed her book and stared. Why was this happening ... again? Why couldn't she have something special that was just hers and hers alone? Everything that she once had as her own, Tiffany was taking away. She was always taking, taking, taking. And now it looked as if she was going to take Uncle Kema too.

Chinella came in to see why Tiffany was giggling so loudly.

'What do you think she'll be then?' Kema asked his sister-in-law. 'When she grows up, I mean.'

'I don't know. I've never really thought about it.'

'Well I have. And I've been there with you when people have talked about Tiffany and the way that she looks and smiles. You can't help but think about it. She's beautiful, Chinella. She'll most probably be a model, don't you think?'

Chinella laughed.

'It's a bit early to start talking like that, isn't it? Still, it's nice of you to say so, Kema.'

Grace was so fed up with this. Didn't they have anything else to discuss but Tiffany? There was no way she could get away from it. Everywhere she turned it was Tiffany, Tiffany, Tiffany. And now *her* Uncle Kema was calling Tiffany beautiful!

The idea of being a model seemed to be scoring Tiffany praise. Well, thought Grace, she wanted some of the same admiration. Uncle Kema had called her pretty once, that meant that she could be a model, too, but when she mentioned it to her mum and Kema they almost laughed at her suggestion. Why? What was so funny about her being a model and not Tiffany?

'It's just,' her mother began to explain carefully, 'that there are certain jobs that only certain people can do . . . or do well and . . .'

'But I could do it, Mummy, look.' Grace picked up the corners of her dress and pinched them between her fingers. As she walked very deliberately, kicking one foot right across the other, she swung her dress from side to side and almost up around her waist. Her attempt to move with style and elegance fell flat and only exposed her stump-like legs and thick knees. Chinella rushed to pull her dress down.

Grace was mortified. She wanted to show everybody, especially Kema, that she could do what was necessary. How dare her mother do that? Maybe she didn't think that it was a good idea for her to be lifting up her dress? It was, after all, showing her knickers, so she'd do it again in a different way.

Grace lifted her right arm, bent her elbow behind her head while putting her left hand on her hip. She wiggled provocatively.

'Grace!' her mother yelled in disgust and astonishment. Grace froze. Her mother's holler had shocked her. She opened her eyes: surely she'd got it right this time? She looked at her uncle for support but Kema looked down at the carpet. 'Stop that now, Grace! Stop it!' hissed Chinella.

Immediately Chinella wanted to retract the way she had dealt with the matter. She had wanted to tell Grace that she could never be a model because she simply didn't have the physical frame, but it had come out all wrong. Shouting at her like that had been of no help to anyone, especially Grace. 'Come here, darling,' Chinella began in an attempt to downplay her initial reaction. 'Look, what I'm trying to say to you is this. There are just certain jobs that some people can't do, and some that they can. Modelling's a possibility for Tiffany, isn't it, Kema? And that's because Tiffany's got what it takes.' Kema looked up and silently agreed with a slow nod of the head. 'But . . . remember what your dad always says, it actually doesn't matter what job you do as long as you become a success, and it's up to you to determine what that success is. You can achieve whatever you want with the abilities that you have. Isn't that right, Kema?'

'Well, Tiffany is stunning, but Grace, you have other qualities.'

Yet whatever they said, somehow Grace still felt inferior. Did they mean that there were some jobs that Tiffany could do but that she didn't have the same options? Her dad had talked about her being a success, but he meant her school work. Well that wasn't enough.

Why wasn't Tiffany just as plump as she was? And why didn't Tiffany wear glasses like she had always had to? And why didn't Grace have those same dimples that looked so sweet and innocent on Tiffany? And why . . . oh but anyway, even if there *were* some differences, it didn't mean that her mother, father, Uncle Kema or anyone else should show favouritism in the way they did. It didn't mean that her mum should spend much more time with Tiffany. That wasn't right, and it certainly wasn't fair.

Then, almost in the way that a black cloud lifts to reveal a clear blue sky, a new vision began to dawn on Grace. Maybe it wasn't their fault. As she thought about it more and more, she realised it couldn't be their fault. Just like the children at her school, they were victims of a child who, like Grace, was using something that she had been given naturally to get what she wanted. This was all down to Tiffany, always crying to get attention, always putting on a show, always smiling that sickly smile so that people said, 'Ahh, isn't she cute.' It was all done to get attention and it worked. And the most frustrating realisation was that, unlike Grace's own stage-managed escapades at school, it had taken Tiffany no effort at all to achieve what she wanted. None.

On top of everything, now her Prince Charming was gone too. In the year since that dreadful day, Kema had met and married a tall, slim Nigerian woman and they had gone back to Nigeria to live. And, Grace decided, he was gone from her heart now too. If ever there was a traitor to her affections, it was him. He'd always spoken about

Tiffany with too much adulation and love in his eyes. How could he have loved both of them that way? What he and Grace had had together, before Tiffany came along, was special. It wasn't meant to be shared with Tiffany or any other woman.

The news of his marriage shouldn't have been so upsetting, but she couldn't control her feelings. It broke her heart and she cracked, crying for hours. She had been getting ready for her birthday party, which turned out to be an unhappy affair since the one person she wanted to be there wasn't. There were lots of screaming children playing pass the parcel and musical chairs, but Grace wasn't interested. Everyone asked her what was wrong but she was numb to their enquiries. How could she reasonably explain that the balloons, cakes and presents brought for her meant nothing, and that it was only her uncle's love that she wanted? Who would understand? Well, it didn't really matter now. All she knew was that her sister was to blame for everything, including the way that she felt, because Tiffany had come along and taken up his time. Grace had concentrated on monitoring this treachery and as a result she'd lost sight of other opposition and allowed Kema's new bride to carry off her prize right under her nose. Well at least now he couldn't marry Tiffany. Now neither of them could have him, but that didn't make Grace feel better. Was this a lesson for later life? Did it mean that if there was a man you wanted, who captured your heart, then you should always go all-out to get him before someone else did? She'd have to remember this. It could prove to be a valuable lesson.

It was always the same. Her mum wouldn't even ask her for an explanation as to why she had done what she did to Tiffany. Wasn't she even worth a question any more? It was ages since she'd had to make up a lie about Tiffany taking her toys or sweets in order to justify her actions. Now her mum didn't even bother to ask.

'Grace? Your room. Go!' Grace didn't move. She didn't have to and, anyway, the longer she stayed there, the longer her mother would be looking in her direction. At least that was something. At least she would be getting some kind of attention. When was the last time her mother had picked her up and cuddled her like she was doing to Tiffany now? She wasn't too big for that. It just wasn't fair.

'Did you hear what I said, girl!?' her mother screamed very loudly. 'Move!' Grace jumped at the volume of her mother's command and ran to her room.

'What's wrong, Chinella?' Falmi came home from work to find his wife with Tiffany snivelling in her arms.

'It's Grace again. Look.' Chinella raised Tiffany's arm to show Falmi the mark. 'What is wrong with that girl? I really don't know what's going to happen to her. Why is she doing this all the time? Why is she turning into some sort of . . . animal?'

Grace pressed close to her bedroom door so that she could eavesdrop. If she was going to be smacked by her father, she wanted advance warning.

'I don't understand it,' her mother was saying. 'I really don't understand what causes her to explode like that. It doesn't make sense because there's just no consistency. When I mentioned her behaviour at home to her form teacher, Mrs Court was really surprised and said that it certainly didn't tally with her behaviour with the other pupils at school. There, she's great. She gets such good social reports. So what happens when she comes home?'

'I think that we're going to have to face it, Chin.'

'Face what? Oh, not this jealousy thing again?'

'Well, that's the only thing that makes sense.'

'I refuse to draw that conclusion. Tiffany and Grace are sisters. There's no competition between them.'

'You mean that there shouldn't be, but there is and it's gone beyond normal sibling rivalry. It's developing into a major problem.'

'Oh, don't exaggerate. I mean it's bad but it's not *that* bad. Grace is just going through a strange stage at the moment. She'll get over it. We just need to get her interested in something. Take her mind off Tiffany.'

'Like what? What could she possibly do?'

'Dr Sapper said that it might be her diet and I should take a look at that.'

'Don't be silly. She eats the same as us, doesn't she? I don't go biting your arm or scratching your face every two seconds of the day. Mind you, maybe Dr Sapper is right in one way. She eats just as much as me, if not more. Maybe it wouldn't be such a bad idea to put her on a diet.'

'Falmi!'

'Well, she is getting a bit . . . a bit fat. Oh, I don't know. I don't know what to suggest any more. I'm all out of ideas.'

'So what do we do?'

Like I said, heaven only knows. I think that you're right, we have to find her an interest.

'But what?'

Falmi shook his head and sighed. 'Well . . . I suppose there is at least one thing to be grateful for,' he said finally.

'What's that?'

'She's always been clever . . . I mean, I don't think that Tiffany's going to become a rocket scientist, or successful in any other way academically, but Grace might . . .'

'What do you mean?'

'School. At least Grace gets really good marks and is doing well.'

'Umm.'

'Umm? What do you mean, umm?'

'Well, while her behaviour isn't bad at school, the standard of her work is slipping ... quite dramatically.'

'But you were at the parents' evening last week. No wonder you were so adamant about me not finishing my shift early and coming with you. How on earth could you keep something like that to yourself? Why didn't you tell me?'

'Because I know how proud you are of her school work and I'm sure that it's just a phase she's going through. I mean, you're always bragging about her test results to your friends.'

'So are you.'

'Yes, I know. I'm proud of what she's achieving at school, well I was, it's just a pity that ...'

'That what? You see, there is a problem and you know what's causing it, but you just don't want to admit it. And while you're doing that, while you're covering it up, the problem is affecting her learning. Something has to be done about it otherwise Grace will start failing in the only arena that she could ever be successful in. Look, it's jealousy, Chinella. Jealousy. Pure and simple.'

Jealousy! Grace didn't want to hear any more. Jealousy? There was no way she was jealous of her little sister. Jealous of what exactly? She was the older one, she was cleverer, taller. What did she have to be jealous of? She kicked her door shut with the sole of her foot. Her parents had got it all wrong. She was acting this way for a reason. Tiffany had been allowed to use her looks to get whatever she wanted, but her manipulations just weren't working.

Yet look at the way that Tiffany was able to turn things around without even saying a word. It was amazing. Well, she wasn't going to win this one. Grace was going to be a success in the very way that her dad had expected. She'd have to start thinking about getting back in favour with her parents in a totally different way now.

It had been a year since the day Uncle Kema had

shown his true colours and a year since she had been forced to show hers, and in that time she'd forgotten her golden rule. In her pain, she'd forgotten that her enjoyment of manipulation came from no-one knowing that she was behind an incident; in her absolute thirst for attention, her hurt over Kema and misery over Tiffany, she'd forgotten to remain behind the scenes. Well, she'd have to rectify that from now on. She still felt that she had every reason to continue her crusade against Tiffany, every reason still to resent her, because everything she was going through right now was Tiffany's fault. But now she was wiser. She couldn't let anybody know that she didn't like her little sister. Quite clearly that wasn't working. It wasn't winning her any points and that was what it was all about. To be successful, you had to be the best. In achieving success, she would then be the one that everybody talked about. The one that everybody liked. Grace lay on her bed plotting and it wasn't long before she felt she had cracked it. It was so simple, and her parents had actually given her the answer. To get back on top was well within her powers and she had already proved that no-one, especially Tiffany, could compete with her in this particular arena.

From that point on, Grace excelled in her school work. Once again her parents were really proud of her achievements and she even represented the borough in school academic competitions. This was a brand new Grace. Gone was the scheming child who appeared bitter and jealous towards Tiffany. In her place was an ever-helpful, ever-caring girl. The conversation she had overheard between her parents had made her realise that she couldn't be seen to be abusive towards Tiffany and she certainly shouldn't leave visible signs of her abuse. She must appear to be kind and loving. On the other hand, she had to prevent Tiffany from being seen to be a success. It was a doddle, and devising ways to execute her scheme was the reason why God had given her a brain. It just so happened that her brain was better than most, especially Tiffany's.

And so Grace's plans to present Tiffany as an under-achieving delinquent were launched. It was easy, especially since she was asked to pick up where her mum had left off. Once Tiffany knew the basics, Grace was asked to continue to teach her how to broaden her reading, writing and arithmetic. It was so easy for Grace totally to confuse Tiffany, misspelling words that she had to learn, mixing up multiplication with division, telling her that teachers weren't allowed to tell you off, so if any of them did, you were allowed to shout back at them.

Grace grew into a shining example of what a twelve-year-old should be, studious, hard working and happy, but by the age of seven Tiffany had become a teacher's worst nightmare and no-one could understand why this seemingly bright girl had taken such a turn for the worse. 'Surely Grace is the best role-model that you could ever need? All that we want you to be is successful, in your own terms. Different people need different things out of life. Your success doesn't have to come academically, but in whatever you do, please always give it your best shot.' These were the last words that Chinella told Tiffany before going out to visit friends one winter's evening in 1969.

The snowflakes were falling thickly on the windscreen, obscuring normal vision, but if only the driver in the blue van had indicated before pulling out, Falmi would have been able to slow down in time. Instead, he had to swerve sharply. The icy surface under his tyres made the car swing out of control into the lane of oncoming traffic, and Chinella's screams echoed through the streets of Ealing.

A photograph of the four-car pile-up was splashed on

the front page of nearly every Fleet Street newspaper the next day. Some of them used it to champion a call for the compulsory wearing of seat belts, for there were no survivors in any of the vehicles.

3

Islington, London, 1973

'What's the time? He's late. That's it. I'm not waiting any more. I'm not going.'

Marcia Abiola's mother sounded perfectly calm, in contrast with the way she was viciously flicking off her high-heeled shoes, sending them flying down the passageway. When the front doorbell rang, Cela called out to Marcia to answer it and inform her date that she was no longer available that evening.

Bassey towered over Marcia as she opened the door. He stood with a bunch of red roses in his hand and an expression of great satisfaction on his face. His black trousers swung above his ankles exposing fluffy red socks too thick to fit neatly into his high-gloss leather shoes.

'Hello, Marcia. Shall I come in or is your mum coming straight out?' He put all his weight on one leg as he leaned to one side, looking past Marcia.

'Mum says she's not going out. Sorry, Mr Ijomanta.'

'What d'you mean she's not going out? I've already booked. And I've got tickets for the dance later as well.

And I've bought her these flowers. Where is she? Is she in? Is she ill?'

'No, Mr Ijomanta, she's not ill.'

'Then what's wrong with her?'

'There's nothing wrong with her, Mr Ijomanta. Nothing at all.'

'Then what is it? Cela!' Bassey blasted down the corridor. 'Cela!' He tried to make some headway past Marcia, but Marcia knew better than to give him even an inch. She'd been through this with so many men so many times before. Mum would not like him to come in and when she was in this sort of mood, it was best that he stayed on the other side of the front door.

Bassey couldn't understand what the problem could possibly be. He'd been there only the night before, the whole night. Was it something he'd done – or hadn't done – before he left that morning? 'What's wrong with her, Marcia?'

Oh no, not one of those. There were certain men who were weak, her mother had always warned her. 'Just look into their eyes,' she'd instructed. 'Unlike a woman, you can always see weakness in a man's eyes and you must steer clear of all of them, Marcia. They can do nothing for you but bring you down to their level.' And this one? Mr Ijomanta? The man in front of her, holding flowers and love in his heart for her mother, a woman who had nothing but scorn and contempt for him, was weak. Marcia was becoming an expert. This one deserved everything he was about to receive if he didn't shift himself from her doorstep. He was about to start whimpering and begging for reinstatement in her mother's affections and another chance, which was a shame because she knew that in her mother's mind he had already bitten the proverbial dust. Yet this man had only just met her mum, so how and why . . . why was he already showing tell-tale signs of such great weakness? Was he weak when her mother met him? He couldn't have been, because she wouldn't have been attracted to him in the first place. So how did her mum manage to get that amount of power over him in such a short time?

'Mr Ijomanta, I told you, there's nothing wrong with my mother.' Marcia looked directly into Bassey Ijomanta's eyes. She had to tell him straight. She'd been on the doorstep long enough and she had two essays to finish for her English homework. She couldn't afford to waste time breaking the news gently.

'It's you,' she admitted. 'You're the problem.'

'Me? Why? What have I done?!'

'You're late.'

'I'm . . . ?' Bassey grappled with the flowers in order to look at his watch. 'I'm not late. I was supposed to be here at eight and it's only twenty-two minutes past. I've been talking to you for . . .'

Oh, boy. Here we go. Excuses, excuses, Marcia predicted.

'. . . for ten minutes, plus . . . anyway . . . there was so much traffic on the way, and, not only that, I had to stop off to buy her these flowers, and, look . . . Cela!'

This was his last plea as he called out to her in the hope that she would take mercy on him and go ahead with the night of entertainment he had planned. He knew that Cela liked a good night on the town. She was a real party girl, but classy. It wasn't going to be a cheap night out for him, but he was more than willing to pay.

It looked like it was working. It looked to Bassey as if Cela had finally heard his calls and was coming towards him in a red sequinned dress ready for their evening out, but Marcia knew differently. She'd been around on many a similar occasion and she began to back away from the door as she waited for the inevitable.

'These are for you, Cela,' were the last words that Marcia heard Mr Ijomanta say.

'Thank you,' Cela said, cradling the flowers in her right arm as she took hold of the side of the door, swinging it with such ferocity that it shook as it slammed shut in Bassey's face. Marcia looked at her mother. Was her reaction really necessary? Had being twenty-two minutes late been *that* bad?

'Why are you looking at me like that? Don't you dare feel sorry for him! The stupid man made me rush home from work, get dressed, put on full make-up and all so that he could be late and I have to take all of this off again? Look, if I've told you once I've told you a million times, Marcia. Men! They're useless! Don't *ever* feel sorry for them. They'll pick that up as a sign of weakness and use it against you. Just use them to get what you want and then lose them. And certainly don't take any of their crap! I had to learn the hard way. Don't ever be like me . . . or my mother!'

Who exactly was her mother's anger directed at? All men? Of all colours? Or was it just the ones who turned up late, wouldn't buy her expensive gifts, had wives or weren't any good in bed? That was the list Cela had given her daughter in order for her to identify no-hopers. But the circle of no-hopers was growing and now seemed to include any man who breathed.

For years Marcia had been aware of the way her mother treated men. She'd seen wine thrown over a couple and she'd sat with her mum in the dark to avoid others standing outside ringing the doorbell, but Marcia noticed that these men would always come back for more. Why? She had no doubt that, in the cold light of day, Mr Ijomanta would try to do the same.

Only now did Marcia even begin, or want, to understand what all her mother's talk about sex and men meant. Now, growing older, she wanted the know-how because she could see that, whatever the environment, it was best to be in control.

Cela had always encouraged Marcia to speak her mind and she wasn't at all surprised at the piercing questions her eleven-year-old daughter had suddenly started firing at her. Cela had deliberately always been open about her own life story, including the ups and downs in her relationships. She felt that it was up to her as a mother to give as much information as possible to enable her daughter to avoid life's pitfalls. The alternative, Cela believed, was for her daughter to remain ignorant, and ignorance had led Cela to the position that she was in now – a single parent. 'Is that what you want to be? Ignorant? It makes no sense sitting there in limbo, girl!' Cela would taunt. 'Don't ever be shy. Tell me what's on your mind. I can see that something is. Come on. Spit it out or forever remain uninformed.' Marcia had no choice but to do just that; she learned not to be backward in coming forward. 'That's what it's all about, Marcia. Life is about knowledge and knowledge, just like sex, is power. So never be afraid to speak, never be afraid to ask and always say what is on your mind.' That suited Marcia, because of late there were always things on her mind.

While Cela and Marcia had an understanding, a relationship in which they talked a lot when they were together, they hardly ever were. They lived together but, emotionally, they were far apart. Cela worked and generally got home at about seven in the evening. Marcia was a latch-key kid who as young as eight was fixing her own meals and devising her own forms of entertainment. She had to, because when Cela wasn't out working she was in her bedroom getting ready to go out and party, or entertaining one of her boyfriends. There were three things that seemed to be important to Cela Abiola, three things that seemed to make her happy – work, socialising and sex.

Work was very important. It gave her the financial independence which was her key to freedom. Her key to not having to put up with anything or do anything for anybody unless she wanted to, and that was rare. Although she was the mother of a young child, she was living her own life. She felt that her duty as a mother ended once she'd put Marcia to bed and having a child didn't mean that you were forever housebound. Oh no. She knew that any child born needed love and attention; but she had to be honest, she had no love to give.

As an only child of parents who did not know how to show her an ounce of love, Cela knew she was not an instinctive mother and she had sworn to herself that she would never bring a child into a world that she regarded as unpleasant and unjust.

Her first negative images of men were formed as a result of being the recipient of her father's anger. A very strict disciplinarian, he punished her quite unreasonably for not emptying the bin on a certain day or not washing his clothes to his impossibly high standard. She was totally responsible for cooking family meals from the age of nine, since both her parents worked. She arrived home from school at four-thirty and the meal had to be prepared and ready for seven, when her father came home. Failure in any respect, unfinished meals, receiving anything less than a B in school tests, questioning her father's decisions, resulted in him using designated leather straps or thick tree branches, beating her soft skin and causing welts to develop all over her body. Although they had faded, she still had some of the scars. Her mother never did a thing to stop him. Cela had never been able to work out whether she was weak or just dumb.

Cela's parents had sent her to England to study at the age of eighteen in the hope that she would become an academic genius, a success. That was all important to her father and his Nigerian pride. She'd been to university, obtained her degree in American History and had not been able to find work related to her speciality, but against strong parental pressure she had decided not to return to Nigeria. She told them that England, as they believed, was the land of opportunity and she had to stay to become successful. She argued that she wouldn't be able to achieve in Nigeria what she could attain if she stayed in England. She knew the key word for her father was success. If she could convince him that that was her goal, she knew that he would give her permission to stay.

She was determined never to return to her father's harsh domination. Even though in reality she was living a lowly life in England, compared with her upper-class existence in Nigeria, her small room and low wages were tantamount to having once been famished and then stumbling across a food mountain. For once in her life she had freedom, for once in her life she was in total control and she was going to celebrate this autonomy. All she had to do was sort out what she wanted and what she didn't. There was certainly plenty of choice and plenty of men.

But things quickly turned sour. Her parents stopped sending her money since she'd pretended to be financially solvent. She couldn't find any work related to her ability and ended up accepting a job as a filing clerk. She had moved from rented room to rented room, and during a brief liaison with an Australian salesman eleven years earlier, she had accidentally fallen pregnant. After Marcia was born all that she could afford was a two-bedroom flat in a large run-down house in Islington. Cela's landlady helped her out with childminding for a nominal fee while Cela continued to work. Money was always tight and her emotions were always running high.

Now, as an attractive thirty-four-year-old woman, she intended to reap justice from the whole of mankind. And she had a right to. It had always been the same, throughout her life. Men had used and abused her. Even though she'd continued to put her trust in them, taken them at face value, hung on to their every supposedly honest word, she had never come up trumps. Like her mum she'd tried being sweet, demure and weak, all the qualities she believed a man would want, but all that attracted was the same sort of men, bastards – bastards like her father, or men who were just out to have a good time . . . at her expense. Her Australian boyfriend had promised her the earth. He'd told her he loved her, said that they would emigrate to his homeland, said that she could always rely on him to be around. He promised her marriage, a happy life together, but all that he delivered was his sperm to make her baby girl. And then he'd gone back to Australia. She'd given birth to Marcia alone, brought her up as a single parent and would never trust another man again. And as for her father – there was no way that she was going to tell her parents about Marcia. No way! For a start, that would mean she had failed. She couldn't have her father gloating over that, especially after she had put up such a fight to stay in England and vowed that she would be a success. Secondly, the mess that she had found herself in was *her* mess; she would deal with it herself. And thirdly and most importantly, any hell that she was experiencing living in London, even if it did include being tied to a helpless child she didn't really want, was far more pleasant than what she would have to face living with her father back home. She'd moved several times now and had not been in contact with her parents for over ten years.

Cela worked for two solicitors, Cintra Arnold and Elvin Douglas, in a small firm on Islington High Street, two minutes from where she lived. Cintra would often call and leave messages with Marcia to tell Cela to call her as soon as she arrived back from work. Cela always complained about this. As far as she was concerned, work was done at work. Cintra Arnold had no right to call her as often as she did at home on work-related matters. More often than not, whatever Cintra wanted, be it to ask where a certain file was or how to work the new switchboard system, could easily have waited until the next day. Sometimes Cela would have to go back to the office having only just arrived home. She complained to Marcia that she was good at her job and that this woman was taking liberties, but she also explained that she was not in a position to do anything about it. This woman was her boss and being the boss meant that she called the shots. So Marcia learned another lesson. There was no joy in being an employee. You had to be at the top to be in control. But how did you get there?

Every morning at eight-fifty at the Alfred Christ School the bell sounded and children gathered in their form rooms to take registration. In Marcia's class, as they sat behind their designated desks, the pupils' attention was always directed at their tutor, Mr Lovett. Here was another lesson to be stored up for the future. She calculated that in what Mr Lovett was doing, taking registration, he was important not just because he was an adult, not just because he was a teacher, but because he was the one standing up front and therefore in control.

Then there was Mrs Bleach. Every Monday the whole school gathered in a large assembly to sing hymns and be brought up to date with issues related to the school. On a platform at the front of the large dining hall where they all sat was a vacant chair left for Mrs Margaret Bleach, the headmistress. Mrs Bleach entered the hall after everybody else had taken their seats when, on cue from the deputy head, everyone would stand almost in salute of Mrs Bleach's presence. As she watched this, Marcia learned once more that it was important to be up there at the front. She wanted to have the power to be able to make people stand when she entered, or look in her direction when she spoke. If you had the power, you were in control and control meant time and attention, both of which were certainly lacking in her life. She continued to take note of everything that went on around her at school and at home. She became aware of what she wanted to do and where she needed to be in the future. It was all very clear. She'd have to work her way up the ladder to the top. She wanted to succeed where her mother had failed. She wanted power, she wanted control and she wanted success. It was her mission in life and her mum was testimony to the fact that it wasn't just about brains. You had to have a plan of action, work hard and, quite clearly, it was then down to the individual to succeed . . . by any means necessary. She wasn't afraid of work. She wasn't afraid to ask questions. She wasn't afraid to step on anyone's toes, if need be, and she wasn't afraid to use her natural attributes as a woman in order to get whatever she wanted out of life. As long as it was on her terms, that she was the user rather than the used, that was OK. She knew that getting to the top wasn't necessarily going to be easy, but not being there wasn't a position she was prepared to contemplate.

4

Brixton, 1975

Tiffany sat in the bath, lathering her body and humming 'My Boy Lollipop', which was one of her favourite tunes. She stretched out and for a while she smiled to herself, relaxing in the warm water. But then, as always, her smile disappeared as those same emotions that had seemed to haunt her whole life resurfaced. It didn't take anything special to trigger them. Memories accumulated in her mind. She could not banish the images. Images of her sister, Grace, and the feelings of horror and loneliness that had followed the news and eventual grim realisation that her parents had been killed in the car crash six years ago.

It should have been a time when the sisters came together, offering emotional support and comfort to each other, but instead she had endured nothing but torment. She remembered how Grace had instantly turned back into a nasty bitch, how she had tried to make Tiffany feel useless, and almost succeeded. They had been taken into care, which Tiffany had always resented, and she was forever getting into trouble in the home. Grace, on the other hand, had appeared almost serene and very well-behaved. She had grown into a large girl, plain to look at if not downright ugly, and she still seemed to resent Tiffany's natural beauty. She was extremely studious, continuing to do well at school, different, in fact, to her younger sister in every way.

While she was perfectly intelligent, Tiffany was more interested in material things. Like any normal young girl, she scanned the fashion magazines, copied the models, sang to herself in the mirror holding curling tongs as a microphone and avidly watched television programmes depicting wealth, fashion and high society.

Grace still disliked her. Tiffany often wondered whether Grace behaved as she did towards her because it was her way of handling the loss of their parents, to hit out at the person closest to her. But that didn't tie in with all the abuse she had to suffer when her parents were alive. Why was Grace still so hostile? Grace was now the one who everybody talked about. She was always the one in the spotlight.

Whatever the reason, Tiffany knew that Grace was certainly aware that what she was doing was wrong because she always hid her actions. She made sure that nobody knew about what she did to Tiffany and on the few occasions when Tiffany complained or showed the bruises, nobody believed Grace was responsible. Worse, everyone in the home assumed Tiffany was pointing the finger at Grace because she didn't like her.

Apart from planting things on Tiffany that she had stolen from around the home deliberately to get her into trouble, Grace continually hit her sister and forced her to steal things from shops. It went on and on until one day Tiffany decided she had had enough. She had taken as much as she could handle and tonight she was going to confront her big sister as soon as she got home from work. She might be only thirteen but she had to make a stand against Grace. In the six years since her parent's death she hadn't been able really to discuss the way she felt about it with anyone. There was so much that she and Grace could be sharing. They should have been making up for the love they were missing from their parents by giving it to each other. Tonight, Tiffany decided, she was going to try to really talk to Grace.

At eighteen, Grace had a room of her own in the home. She had left school and was working as a wages clerk in the accounts department at British Airways. When she got back that night, Tiffany would be waiting in her room in the hope that she could put an end to all the aggression she'd had to face from her sister.

Grace usually got back at six-thirty in the evening, but not that night. Tiffany sat there waiting, nervously rehearsing the appeal she was going to make to the better nature of her older sister, wondering what sort of response she was going to get and knowing that, if it failed, it would be their last chance ever to have a proper, loving, sisterly relationship.

The seconds, minutes and hours ticked by but still Grace didn't come home. Finally, at ten o'clock, Tiffany reluctantly decided that the special reunion she so longed for was not going to happen that night. She opened the door to leave and then she heard the sound of her sister's voice down the corridor.

But what Tiffany didn't realise was that Grace had accepted a date with someone from her office. It was their first date. Kevin was tall, white, fat and much older than Grace. He worked in the same office and they had met earlier in the evening at Grace's request. They had gone to a pub and Grace's behaviour there left Kevin in no doubt as to what she wanted. Kevin told Grace that he just wanted to make sure she got home to bed safely. Grace had instigated the evening, she knew exactly what he wanted and, first date or not, she would give it to him.

She wasn't a virgin but it wasn't too often that she got this type of attention from a man.

As they entered Grace's room Kevin backed Grace up against the door, closed it and, holding her hands high above her head, started to kiss and bite her neck. They hadn't noticed Tiffany who was curled up in the armchair, too embarrassed to speak. This wasn't at all what she had been expecting. Grace was supposed to burst in, notice that her light was on, see Tiffany sitting in her armchair and ask her what the hell she wanted. Tiffany would then pour her heart out and, after hearing her confessions and understanding what she had been going through, Grace would hug her and tell her everything was going to be OK.

But Grace only noticed Tiffany when Kevin began to pull her towards the bed.

'Umm, Kevin,' Grace nodded towards Tiffany, 'we've got company.'

Tiffany got up, edging backwards towards the door. At thirteen her breasts were still small but she was tall, beautiful and looked old for her age.

'Who's this?' Kevin asked. Tiffany knew instantly that he was drunk.

'Oh, just one of the younger ones from the home,' Grace said quickly. 'Go on, run along, Tiffany.'

'No, Tiffany. Hold on a minute.' Kevin looked at her admiringly. 'Come here. Come and say hello.' He walked over to her and blocked her way by leaning an arm against the wall and standing in her path. Tiffany froze.

'Are you crazy?' Grace snapped. 'I'm taking a big enough risk having you here as it is. You can't muck about with the youngsters.'

But Kevin just grabbed at Grace and nuzzled drunkenly at her large breasts while his hand went under her skirt.

'What are you doing, Kevin?'

He kissed her and then pushed her back roughly,

turning his attention to Tiffany. Suddenly all the familiar bitter emotions surfaced in Grace. Here we go again, she thought. Tiffany was stealing what was rightfully hers. Just like the attention from her parents, the comments from passers-by and the love of her Uncle Kema. Grace could see what Kevin was up to. The way that he was playing with Tiffany's hair and tugging at her clothes quite clearly meant he wanted to fuck her. There he was, her man even though it was only their first date, trying to get it on with her sister. Well, Tiffany had to learn once and for all that messing with Grace's possessions was as deadly as messing with fire. OK, if Tiffany wanted Kevin, she could have him. Grace would stand by and do nothing. Actually, watching Tiffany wriggle and try to get away was turning her on. What was the stupid girl doing in her room anyway?

Grace had to move her legs out of the way quickly when Kevin pushed Tiffany on to the bed.

'Grace! Tell him to stop. Grace!'

Kevin looked at Grace. If he had received any indication that he should stop, he would have. But all he saw was Grace's smile.

Kevin fumbled with Tiffany's clothes. She began to scream, and Kevin slapped his hand over her mouth as he worked his lips down her slim body. Tiffany's screams grew louder. Instead of going to her sister's aid, Grace put on a Jackson Five tape and turned the volume up loud enough to drown the screams. Now Kevin could put the hand that had been smothering Tiffany's screams to better use.

The image that would stay with Tiffany for the rest of her life was of the smile on Grace's face as she flicked the light switch and plunged the room into darkness, leaving her little sister alone to be raped.

Tiffany tried to suppress the anguish and the confusion

that welled up inside her each time she thought of that night but she felt so dirty, so abused. No matter how long she spent scrubbing her body in the bath she just didn't feel clean. She couldn't come to terms with what her sister had allowed to happen to her. Every time Tiffany came into contact with Grace after 'that night', she simply couldn't look at her. What Grace used to do to her was bad enough, physically abusing her for no reason at all, but to have been involved in her losing her virginity to a drunken slob. For her sister to have given her blessing to her rape! To Tiffany, Grace had committed an act of total betrayal for which there could never be forgiveness. But right now she was a teenager without a voice. Given her supposed bad behaviour in the home and the way Grace was bathed in glory, who could she tell? Who would believe her? Who would ever think that Grace would condone such a disgusting act?

There was Linda, the social worker who had been assigned to the two of them. But Linda had already shown a bias towards Grace on more than a few occasions. Tiffany couldn't trust her with this; Linda wasn't the one to turn to. She thought about the police . . . but what would they do? After talking to staff at the home they would most probably conclude that she had had sex with someone of her own accord, regretted it and was now blaming her sister for her major indiscretion. They'd want to examine her, question him, and on top of everything Grace's behaviour toward her would be worse than ever.

Tiffany couldn't deal with that. She'd had as much as she could take. So just four days after the incident, still unable to come to terms with what had happened, Tiffany ran away from the home.

She spent eight days on the streets of London. At night, London was a beautiful city. Piccadilly Circus seemed to come alive with subliminal invitations to all passers-by to forget their personal troubles and be happy, but they weren't for Tiffany. She walked aimlessly, her vision often blurred by tears. No-one asked her why she was crying. No-one noticed, no-one cared. What had she done to deserve this? She couldn't think of anything bad enough to mean that she should be without a family. Without a home. Without anyone to love her. Without anyone to talk to, anyone to care. She had loved her parents, especially her mum. Why had God decreed that she should have this sort of life and taken theirs away? For her, no more school. No family. She was on her own.

By night she avoided inspectors and managed to sleep in London railway stations. It was cold, lonely and frightening, but anything was better than the situation she had run away from. She'd taken the money she had managed to save up at the home, eight pounds, but she soon discovered that it didn't go very far.

Each morning she would go to the station's toilets and have a wash. One day a cleaner told her she could get a shower very cheaply at the local swimming baths. Tiffany was embarrassed that the cleaner was aware of her circumstances, but she took her advice.

And it was here that she met Perry, who was to become the father of her child.

Perry Walker was eighteen and exceptionally good-looking, a dead ringer for Billy Dee Williams in the film *Lady Sings the Blues*. He had plenty of common sense and was very street-wise, playing guardian to a group of children aged eleven to fifteen who hadn't all run away from home but occasionally needed 'space' to get away from their parents – or others! If anyone ever asked him why he let such young boys hang around him, he pointed out, 'They don't think for themselves, they don't answer back, they don't want to take over. Actually, do you know what the main reason is?' he expounded on his philosophy. 'Because they need me. Straight up. They need someone like me.

44

I can identify with some of the problems they're having at school or with their parents. And you know what, they trust me,' he ended proudly.

Indeed they did. Tony, for instance, a twelve-year-old boy, had confided in him that he was feeling a lot of pain, a burning sensation every time he took a pee. Perry initially told him to pay more attention to his hygiene and they left it for a while, but a few days later, when there was no improvement and Tony discovered a yellow-coloured discharge, Perry was worried. This sounded serious; it actually sounded like VD. Further interrogation revealed that Tony's uncle was having sex with him on a regular basis, paying him each time. Tony's understanding of the problem was very simple: before he got involved with Perry, he needed the money because his mum never had any, but now that Perry was giving him money he wanted his uncle to stop doing what he was doing. They used to meet at his mum's house when she went to bingo, but now Tony was trying to persuade his uncle to leave him alone. Each time he promised it would be the last but he kept on coming back, time and again, until Perry went to see him.

After that, as if by magic it seemed to Tony, his uncle never, ever returned.

Perry had been left in charge of his mother's council flat while she went to America to pursue a relationship with a compulsive gambler. She swore that she would soon send him an airline ticket so he could join her. That was fourteen months ago. Meanwhile he was making a good living, even though he didn't work – at least not in the conventional way.

Oaktree Swimming Baths was where Perry went for his daily morning swim. Having represented his school in many tournaments, he still kept up his favourite sport. While he was doing his twenty lengths, he was also able to relax, keep fit, collect his thoughts and plan for the day ahead.

Arriving in the hallway one morning, Perry realised he didn't have any change.

'Have you got change of a fiver?' he called out to a girl walking past him.

'Is that a joke? I've got about five pence left to live on. Sorry.' Tiffany began to walk towards the exit. She had just spent almost all she had on a shower.

'Hold on.' Perry quickly ran after her. 'Are you serious?'

'Serious about what?'

'The money you've got to live on?'

Who was this guy asking her questions? Personal questions. Tiffany had always had her pride. She didn't have to tell him a thing, but, on the other hand, what did she have to hide? It wasn't her fault that she was in this predicament. 'Yeah. Yes I am,' she said reluctantly.

'Well, here.' Perry offered her the five-pound note. 'I don't need it.'

Tiffany studied him with surprise and then suspicion. 'Do you usually go around handing money to strangers? What are you expecting me to do for it?' She noticed he was really good-looking, like the men in the American magazines that she used to love. What was he, a pimp? Trust was something Tiffany had very little of.

'Where are your parents? Your family? Where do you live?' Perry began, but then he picked up on her feelings of suspicion and decided to take a more sympathetic line. 'I'm not expecting anything in return . . . nothing. Look, I've got a feeling that you may be in trouble and I can help you . . . if you'll let me.'

Tiffany looked at him. She had nothing to lose. She would go with him. Maybe at last here was someone she could trust.

5

Kent, March 1976

Their wedding was one of the biggest that year, paid for by Clare's father, Sir Graham Moot, a gynaecologist to the rich and famous with his own prestigious private practice in Harley Street. Everyone who was anyone in the medical field was invited, if not to the ceremony then to the reception which took place in the Grand Hotel ballroom, in London's Park Lane.

One hundred tables were set out in a rectangular shape, each seating eight, lavishly covered with pink and white lace tablecloths and decorated with flowers. Each place was set with crisp white napkins, sparkling glasses, cutlery and gold-crested plates, and accompanied by a name-plate embossed in gold italic writing. The newly wedded Mr and Mrs Peter Duvall welcomed their guests as they arrived and were announced, before their photographs were taken and they were escorted to their seats.

As the master of ceremonies asked the guests to raise their champagne glasses in a toast to Mr and Mrs Peter Duvall, the fire alarm sounded in the hotel and everyone was asked to vacate the ballroom via the fire exit, and to stand well back in the grounds outside. Clare joked that she hoped this wasn't an omen for their future married life.

Clare's white heels sank into the soft lawn as she stood proudly beside her husband. He was deep in conversation with her father and a group of other doctors whom he was soon to join at St Helen's Hospital in Edgware. It was everything that Clare had ever wanted: to be the wife of a man with such a bright, shining future. Peter was strong in every sense of the word and she felt totally secure with him. He'd passed his degree in medicine at Cambridge University with first-class honours and had just completed the additional exams related to his profession. Already accepted as a junior in the same hospital where his new father-in-law was a senior consultant, and promised a partnership in the future with his lucrative private practice, Peter had told Clare that he was eager to please her father, the person who had made it all possible. And to Graham, Peter was the son he had never had. He was more than pleased when Peter made an appointment to see him to ask for his daughter's hand in marriage – if he hadn't, Graham might well have suggested it to Peter himself. To Graham, Peter was perfect. His parents came from the right, upper-middle-class background, he had the right temperament, was caring, considerate, career-minded and ambitious. And most important, he could see that Peter loved his daughter. Graham Moot was one of the old school. He believed that men were the providers and should always financially support their wives. He wasn't primitive enough in his ideals to stop his daughter from going to university herself, but now it was up to a man to look after Clare. In Peter, he saw the perfect person for that role, someone who could enable Clare to get on with the equally important female task of raising his grandchildren.

To Clare, Peter was also the answer to any woman's

dreams. He was intelligent, good-looking, tall, confident and determined to succeed. They became best friends before they became lovers and gave each other support and real happiness. They forged a strong, healthy relationship and Clare had even been able to convince Peter to give up smoking. She'd sensibly argued, 'How can you be a medical student, specialising in cardiology, and still be a smoker? It doesn't make any sense at all. What kind of example are you going to be setting your patients?'

They were known as the beautiful couple. Clare was tall and slim. She wore her auburn hair long and straight, flattering her soft features, slim nose, expressive mouth and wide hazel eyes. Her eyelashes were long and curled up towards her thick dark eyebrows. They were both immaculate dressers, preferring designer clothes to Marks & Spencer, champagne to wine, but 10CC to Mozart. But above all they could talk to each other, their conversations often lasting from evening right through to the early hours of the next morning.

Peter was a frequent and popular speaker at Cambridge debates. He was a Conservative through and through, believing in private health care, the reintroduction of capital punishment and the privatisation of all nationalised industries. A career in politics was his real ambition and his ultimate goal in life was to win a seat in the House of Commons. With his new father-in-law's influence he knew he stood more than a chance of achieving his dreams but first he wanted to qualify as a doctor.

Peter believed it was every man for himself. His view was that there had to be a class system in order to keep the country up and running; that the work force had to be led and the leaders needed to be better educated and better paid than the workers, otherwise there could be no respect. He wasn't a racist, believing that a man was as good as his mental ability whatever his skin colour, but he did believe that the reason why the majority of black people (and a certain number of whites) didn't seem to reach their full potential wasn't because they came from different starting points in life, or were discriminated against. Peter thought it had to do with their lack of commitment to work and lack of desire to succeed. He couldn't see that nepotism was playing a crucial part in his career path; he felt that he had done as much as he should do, getting the best grades possible, and that his placement at a hospital even before qualifying would have happened for him anyway. Clare's father was just making things happen faster.

Clare agreed with everything Peter said or did. Like her mother, her only ambition was to be the ideal wife, loving, loyal and totally supportive. Her desires had to be his desires. They could not pull in different directions; there could only be one path to their future and that had to be the one he chose to follow. She put her trust and her life in his hands. He was the captain of their ship and she wanted it that way.

While she was growing up Clare rarely saw her father, except on occasional weekends when he would leave his Harley Street practice and accompanying upstairs flat and spend Saturday and Sunday with his family. She saw that her mother always made a fuss of her father on his return. Her attention was devoted to him, cooking him sumptuous meals, catering to his every need, and Clare could see that this made her father happy and that in turn made her mother so. This, to Clare, was what a happy household and married life was all about.

Clare didn't want much for her future. She was a kind, giving person anyway. All that she hoped for in later life was to be happy, just like her mother, in a secure home with a loving husband. She'd been eager to fall in love, be a good wife and mother, and now she had found the perfect husband in Peter Duvall.

What could possibly go wrong in her life?

Ealing, 1978

It looked as if it was about to pour with rain, thought Tiffany as she peered over the balcony in anticipation of Perry's return.

She watched as Perry and his gang unloaded the stolen goods from the van and carried them up the stairs to the living room of his first-floor flat. It was always easier to carry out burglaries in the dead of night.

Their haul tonight included twenty-six televisions, nineteen stereo systems, countless watches, rings and chains. They knew nothing about high-quality antiques and weren't interested in learning. They stole items to order and picked up any additional objects that they could sell on the grapevine without any hassle. Sometimes they would take the goods to their regular fence who asked no questions, just gave them cash in return, but there was always a stream of men visiting Perry's flat to see what was for sale and to pick up a bargain.

'Can I have this portable?' Tiffany asked, noticing a small black and white ten-inch TV on the floor.

'What do you want that for? We've got one in the bedroom, in fact we've got one in every bedroom.'

'I need one in the kitchen. I can't see the TV in the living room from there when I'm cooking.'

'OK. Take it. Steve, can you make a note of what we've got tonight? No, actually, leave it, I'm really tired. Why doesn't everyone come back in the morning, say ten o'clock, and we can set about seeing who we can sell what to. This time we've got much more than we had orders for.'

'Can I take this for my mum?' asked one of the younger boys, picking up a very expensive-looking ruby and diamond ring.

'Leave it till tomorrow, Tone. We'll sort it out then.'

'But it's her birthday tomorrow. You just let Tiffany take something. Why don't you ever let us have any of the things that we nick?'

'Tiffany took an old black and white portable, that's a bit different. The owner wouldn't even have written down the serial number of that. Look, I've told you before. When we sell the stuff, you can take the money that you're given and buy something. That way you get a receipt.'

'But . . .'

'Tomorrow, Tony. Do you hear me . . . ? Tiffany, can you get me a beer?'

Perry walked away to his bedroom. The other boys started to leave but instead of putting the ring back, Tony slipped it into his pocket. He knew exactly which house it had come from because he had stolen it himself for his girlfriend and he was going to make sure no-one else got hold of it.

Tiffany had lived with Perry as his girlfriend for over three years now. Perry had introduced her to a new life. It was a life of crime but nonetheless she never went hungry, she was never lonely, never wanted for anything. She felt she was successful because success to her wasn't about being a millionaire, the size of the house you lived in, the car you drove or the exams you passed. Success to her was about feeling secure and, although initially she was scared when she realised what Perry did for a 'living', she soon began to find it exciting and grew to rely on it. On one occasion, she had even asked Perry whether she could accompany him and his young friends on their 'rounds', but he had refused her request outright and was amazed and angry that she had even considered it. 'D'you think that I do this for fun?' he had said bitterly. 'It's purely out of necessity. Don't ever get involved in any criminal activities, Tiffany, *ever*, do you understand?'

It reminded her of the film *Oliver* in a way. The gang of five boys met every two or three days to burgle houses and when one of them identified a soft target they would carry out armed robberies, mainly in the West End, jewellery shops and suburban post offices. For burglaries they'd usually go to up-market areas like Chiswick, Richmond, St John's Wood, Finchley and Hampstead.

Perry had two hand guns which he'd acquired in exchange for some jewellery, but he was the only one who carried a gun on their raids; he never allowed any of the boys to have one. He only used a gun when they were robbing post offices, not shops. Tiffany never understood the moral behind that one. When they were 'doing' a jewellery shop they would don balaclavas and then rush in, smash open the glass counters with hammers and grab as much jewellery as they could, aware that an alarm had most probably sounded, if not in the shop, then in a local police station or security office. The getaway car was always stolen the morning before the crime. Their driver would be waiting with a predetermined route to freedom. Once away from the scene of the crime, they were dropped off one by one at different locations and made their own way back to base by public transport. The police would be looking for a gang of five, not individuals travelling on a bus.

Over the past few years their profits had been sufficiently high for Perry to take over the tenancy of his mother's flat, since she wasn't coming back from America. He was doing OK. He drove a BMW 2000TI and had money in the bank, which was more than his mother ever had. He'd even opened a building society account for Tiffany. To her he had become a father, brother, lover and friend all in one. For the first time since her parents died, Tiffany felt secure: she felt that someone really cared for and loved her. She had found her interpretation of success.

There was just one piece missing from the jigsaw. Perry was already in bed sitting up against the headboard.

'Thanks, babes,' he said as she stood by his side and handed him a can of Special Brew. 'D'you want some?'

'No! No ... I don't think that that would be a good idea,' replied Tiffany nervously. 'Umm, actually, I think I'll have a bath before I come to bed.'

'Hey, what's up?'

'Something has to be up because I want to have a bath?'

'Don't be silly. Come here.'

Tiffany took off her shoes and rolled over Perry to get to her side of the bed. She rested her head against the large velvet headboard. Perry put his drink down and turned to her.

'Hey, I know you well enough to know that something's wrong. What is it?' He kissed her forehead gently. Well, here goes, she thought. I wonder how he'll take the news.

All night she'd thought about what his reaction would be, and she'd had several hours to consider how she would tell him. Perry had collected the van for the burglaries from his friend Steve at seven that evening. The deal was that

Steve would get five per cent of the money when they sold the goods. He worked for a car hire firm and regularly had vans and lorries at his disposal, but if anything were ever to 'go wrong' Steve would pretend he knew nothing about it and would say that the van had been stolen because he had carelessly left the keys in the ignition. As long as they both stuck to the same story, the police would have to accept it. But there was no need to think about things 'going wrong'. For years now this was the way Perry had managed to pay the rent and survive. His luck wasn't about to run out now. With Tiffany's new situation, it couldn't . . .

'We've never talked about contraception, Perry. Never. And so I never used any. I mean, I'm not even registered with a doctor or anything yet . . . but you see last month, I didn't have a period right, didn't you notice? So I bought one of those pregnancy tests from the chemist and . . .'

'You're pregnant? You're joking!'

Tiffany closed her eyes tight. Did this mean he was angry?

'That's brilliant. Fucking hell! That's brilliant, Tiffany! Come here. You know that you don't owe me anything, but our own baby is the best gift ever. So? Well . . . what shall we call our baby boy?'

'It might be a girl, Perry, but if it is a boy we'll call him Perry junior.'

'Sounds brilliant to me.'

Tiffany's life was perfect.

7

Cromwell Road, London, 1978

Grace followed her boss to his company car, keeping a few yards behind him in the shadows.

She was desperate for a date but however hard she tried she never had much success.

The underground car park was badly lit, its high ceiling supported by tall, solid concrete blocks which lined the entrance and exits. She almost had him cornered. For now she'd stay out of sight, but this time, he couldn't get away. He couldn't close his office door, say that he was in a meeting or pretend to be otherwise engaged. Right now it was just the two of them and there was no way he was going to get out of it!

While they were coming down in the lift together he'd turned her down for the fifth time. How dare he do that? He'd set up her hopes for a date and let them go with a bang. She really had thought that it was going to happen but he'd left it until the actual day to change his mind, thinking that he could get away with the excuse of a migraine. Wasn't it women who were supposed to suffer headaches and use them as excuses? She'd heard a few of the girls talking about the very same thing in the office just last week. One of them had made up an excuse to fob someone off when she realised that she had double-booked for the evening. Grace never had that problem. Chance would have been a fine thing, two men asking her out on a date for the same day! She would be lucky if she had two men asking her out in the same year, and now, now even her understanding and generous boss was running a mile.

Grace conveniently chose to forget that it had been she who pestered him for a date – over and over again. What in heaven's name was she supposed to do to get a man? Kidnap him? She had no friends. No family. She wanted company and she wanted sex, but now she couldn't even give it away!

Grace was a loyal employee in British Airways' accounts department. It had been nearly four years since she started and not once had she ever been late. She was a conscientious worker who had set her sights on success. Her father had told her the only way she would achieve it was through education but she had left school with eight grade A O-levels and, after landing her post at British Airways, she had no intention of going back to study. She had only really been trying hard at school to please her parents, particularly her father. Since his death, experience had taught her that success came through different things – like marriage or promotion. Even just having a boyfriend would bring her contentment. Right now all she had was her job to enable her to keep her head above water and stay sane.

Kevin had left the company soon after the incident with Tiffany and she blamed her sister for his absence from her life. She believed they could have had a future together and that he had only taken the severance payment offered to certain employees at British Airways because he felt that Tiffany might have told someone about what had happened. Even though he totally ignored her the day after the rape, and for the next six weeks until he left the company, Grace still wanted Kevin and had tried to win him back. She'd written love letters to him and spread rumours through the whole office that they were an item. In reality he *was* scared of the mounting repercussions of his one-night stand, but contrary to what Grace believed it wasn't Tiffany he feared. He didn't even know she was Grace's sister. It was Grace herself who terrified him. She'd already proved herself to be a mad woman in the way she was pursuing him, and what was all of that about anyway? After raping Tiffany, who subsequently ran out of the room, he then had sex with Grace who had been far too demanding for him. In the end he almost had to run out of her room himself. He hadn't come, and he knew that she hadn't either, so what was all this sexual desire about? Why was she so hot on his heels, spouting all this crap about love and a long-term relationship, when he hadn't even been able to keep it up on their one and only night of supposed passion? As far as Kevin was concerned, Grace was too much to handle, leaving aside her large body, decidedly plain looks and offputting personality. He hadn't even fancied her that night when he was drunk and randy, much less in the cold light of day.

But to Grace, Kevin was a lost opportunity. One of her most important goals was marriage and she felt that Kevin could have been the one for her, but she had barely been able to get to first base with him. And all because of Tiffany. If it hadn't been for Tiffany, Grace decided, she could have been in a relationship by now, maybe even married. It was Tiffany's fault that her one and only night of love-making with Kevin had gone so drastically wrong. To this day she'd never learned why her stupid sister had been in the room that night. And it was definitely Tiffany's fault that she now had no real self-confidence and such low self-esteem – it was no wonder she hadn't been able to secure another date in the last three years.

Since her parents died, Grace hadn't been able to move on emotionally. Their death had taken away her opportunity to challenge them about the way she had always felt excluded throughout her childhood. Her feelings hadn't changed. While they were living with their parents and after they were sent to the home, being able to torment Tiffany, physically or mentally, had made her feel as though she was getting something back for the way that everyone around her had made her feel. Now, with everyone gone, she'd been left feeling unwanted and mentally wounded, simmering with negative emotions. With the exception of Linda, the social worker from the home with whom she kept in contact, Grace couldn't talk to anyone. And she couldn't confide in Linda the real reason why Tiffany had run away from the home, so consequently she had to keep a lid on most of her true thoughts and feelings.

Linda could see there was an emptiness in Grace's life and heart. Grace sometimes spoke to her of her feelings about her past life and family and Linda wanted to do something to help. Surely, Linda thought, it was simple at least to try to start putting things right. There was no need for Grace constantly to feel down, especially since all of her misery revolved around being alone in life. As a social worker, Linda had experienced the animosity between many feuding families. More often than not, what was really needed was for those involved to have a safe, controlled arena in which to air their grievances. Not knowing the real reason why Tiffany had run away, Linda felt sure that this was what the girls required to make a start in correcting whatever had gone wrong between them. She wanted to set up a meeting between Grace and Tiffany so they could try to sort out their sibling problems. Quite clearly there was a lack of communication between the sisters. Linda's aim was to get them back together again.

Linda had kept in telephone contact with Tiffany since Tiffany rang her a few months after she ran away to let her know she was safe. She knew that Linda genuinely cared about her, and wanted to put her mind at rest. Linda also visited Grace whenever she could and on one occasion she even accompanied her on a visit to her parents' graves in Streatham Vale. But while Grace welcomed Linda's occasional company, she was far from interested in her idea of a family reunion. However, what Grace didn't realise was just how dangerous her situation was becoming. Because she had no friends, never confided in anyone and kept the lid on her bitterness and resentment tight shut, her emotions were reaching exploding point. She didn't realise that keeping everything bottled inside her was doing her more harm than good. She was fast becoming a sad and desperate figure. She was unaware that her jaundiced feelings towards Tiffany were grossly misplaced. She was unaware that she could take control of her own life and she had no sense of who she really was. Even at this stage in her life, she had analysed that Tiffany was to blame for her complete lack of success. She was also to blame for Grace's feeling that she was really not worth looking at, and not even worth getting to know. Grace felt that she had a lot of love to give but who was there for her to give it to? Her parents were gone, and she had convinced herself, they never loved her anyway. If she had no love from her own parents, how in heaven's name was a stranger going to fall in love with her?

She was well aware that she wasn't liked. Grace had once been in a toilet cubicle when three women from Accounts took their coffee break, standing around the washbasins and gossiping about members of staff. They were particularly cruel about Grace. They talked about her clothes, the way that she seemed to lack colour co-ordination, her sense of style and her weird-shaped shoes. They talked about her hair, the way it was always the same, plaited down the centre of her head, and one even said that she bet, since it sometimes looked a little untidy, that Grace didn't redo it every day and that she'd never seen the inside of a hairdressing salon. They wondered who her friends were exactly. No-one had ever come to meet her at the office and they laughed about her weight and looks. She was at least a size eighteen and the large-framed glasses that she wore only accentuated her roundness. The glasses rested on her chubby cheeks and she regularly removed them to wipe shiny little beads of sweat from her forehead.

Grace had stayed in the toilet for the whole twenty-minute coffee break until the women left. Then she sat on the toilet seat and cried. She cried as long and as hard as she had on the day that Kema left, as long and as hard as the day she learned that her parents had died. She missed her parents so badly. She wanted those days back, she wanted them back because then she had been part of a family, her life had mattered, *she* mattered.

The gush of sentiment and self-pity that Grace experienced made her begin to wonder for the first time whether Linda was right. Had her suggestions about resolving the breakdown between her and Tiffany made sense after all? Should Grace's desire be not to try to forget Tiffany, but to see her again? But would seeing Tiffany really help matters? Probably not. What she actually needed was a positive mental attitude. Maybe today she could do something to change her way of life, because if she didn't take the initiative she would always be in the same old mundane position and Tiffany would have won. Well, she was the first-born. Of the two of them it was up to her to be the first to achieve success.

Generally Grace left her office, in Cromwell Road, south-west London, at five-thirty in the evening. She walked to the Tube station, usually reaching Brixton, where she had a one-bedroom council flat in Coldharbour Lane, by six-fifteen. Each night she went to the fish and chip shop on her way home. She knew that her fatty diet and lack of exercise were telling on her figure, but of late she'd lost the will to do anything about it. Once home, she'd kick off her shoes, curl her legs up underneath her in an armchair and watch TV. Seldom did the phone ring. She'd only had it installed so that she could order pizzas and Chinese takeaways.

When she first moved into the council flat, which was organised by Linda at the home, she'd had so many plans. She had colour schemes in mind and was going to redecorate totally, making it into her own little palace. But of late life had been getting her down. At work she was always diligent but constantly being passed over for promotion. She longed to have a partner but that wasn't happening, and there was never a need to use the social diary that she had bought. She had no hobbies; her spare time was just her, the television and food. So when her boss had offered her his time and attention in order to help with the ledgers for a complicated account, she saw it as an ideal chance to ask him for a date.

Today she had decided to take the step that could change her life. Now, in the car park, before he got into his car, she was going to do it. It had to be now, before she lost her nerve; she'd have to grab this opportunity and see what happened. What was wrong with him coming round to her flat to do the additional work anyway? He'd intimated that he would and now he had backed out. Well, she was fed up with being passed over in that way. She was fed up with being talked about and never talked to. She was a person before she was fat, black or anything else. She had a right to have a relationship.

He spun around as he heard his name. She plastered her thick lips on to his and even when he began beating her off, she didn't let go. She thought that if she just held on tight, just kept on going, he would get used to it and start liking it.

Grace didn't understand it. The next day she was holding a piece of paper with the British Airways letterhead outlining the reasons for her dismissal. She was barred from entering the BA building and her telephone calls to apologise and offer an explanation fell on deaf ears.

Six weeks after she made the pass at her boss in the car park she was experiencing total frustration at the constant rejections for even an interview, let alone a job, with any other company. Unemployment across the country was high, her self-esteem was at its lowest ebb and rapidly turning into depression. She turned to comfort eating and her weight escalated, making her feel even worse. Grace was parentless, sisterless, boyfriendless, friendless and jobless.

Her call to Linda one evening was a last cry for help. Linda again offered the only thing she could see as a solution to Grace's problems.

'You don't have to be alone, Grace. I'm listening to all that you're saying and the one thing you keep coming back to is being on your own in the world. Some people get a lot of comfort from their friends or their partners, but nothing will ever beat ... Look, you know what I'm going to say. You're not alone. You still have a sister out there, Grace. Don't ever forget that. I can contact Tiffany again to see if she would like to see you now or, better still, why don't you write to her? Put down all the feelings that you're talking about now in a letter to her. Let her know that you care and that you want to see her. I'll speak to her too, but do it, Grace. Make sure you write that letter today.'

8

Ealing,
1978

Chantelle Pearl Ideh was born on the sixteenth of October 1978 in Queen Charlotte's Hospital, Hammersmith. Tiffany decided to give Chantelle her own surname since Perry wasn't around to sign the birth certificate.

The past seven months had been very hard. Tony had given the ruby and diamond ring he had taken from their haul to his fourteen-year-old girlfriend, who had showed it to a neighbour without realising she was a policewoman. Everything had come tumbling down. Tony had always been weak and soon he was telling the police all he knew. As a result Perry was arrested.

Perry was usually meticulous about selling on the goods and buying things which were accompanied by a receipt but unfortunately, with their last haul, he simply hadn't had enough time. When the police arrived at Perry's flat the very next morning, they smashed their way into a an Aladdin's cave of stolen delights. Tony and all the other boys faced charges until their ages were revealed, and then the full attention of the investigation focused on Perry.

The police took away everything. They even confiscated Perry's BMW, saying that it had been bought with the proceeds of selling stolen goods, and then they froze his bank account. Unless he could provide proof of income, he wouldn't get anything back. He couldn't. The only thing left was the portable black and white television that Tiffany had put in the kitchen.

Perry's arrest and subsequent imprisonment plunged Tiffany back into the loneliness that she dreaded and had not had to face since she met him three years earlier. The social services tried to help her as much as possible after Perry was arrested. Tiffany told her doctor about her past and her records on the central files showed that she was a runaway. It was decided that, since she had turned sixteen, she could stay where she was in the light of her age and the fact that she'd been living on her own away from the home for so long.

Tiffany decided to keep quiet about her building society account. She would have to try to save that money for when Perry came out. Social services arranged for her to get a grant from the DHSS to pay for essential items like a cot, a pram and bedding. Her rent was paid by them and she received about thirty pounds a week for her upkeep. Social services also left her something else, something she hadn't asked for and didn't particularly want – a contact number for her sister. She was assigned a social worker from her area, Helen, who, along with Linda, advised Tiffany to get in contact with her only other living family member.

'She's very anxious that you get in touch. You say that she's the reason you ran away from the home in the first place, but it's been nearly four years now. And you're sure that you still don't want to talk about it . . . ? Well, we've left the ball in your court and we respect the fact that you don't want us to give her your details, but just remember that blood is thicker than water. You might visit Perry every week but he's going to be away for a very long time, isn't he? I've no doubt that he will be a good father when he comes out but he can't help you right now, can he? With this little one you need all the help you can get. Listen, I've been speaking to Linda again. Did she call you? Grace wanted your number, is it OK to pass it on?' Helen tried to slip it in quickly but Tiffany's horrified expression showed that it hadn't gone unnoticed. Helen tried again. 'Listen, Tiffany, I'm an only child and I would have done anything to have had a brother or sister. You've got one. Don't throw the chance of a reconciliation away. Whatever happened in the past between you should remain in the past. Surely it couldn't have been that bad, Tiffany! You want to do everything you can for Chantelle. You want to be a success as a mother, don't you?'

What does she know? thought Tiffany. What the hell does she know? The only person who knew about the rape her own sister had condoned was Perry. Tiffany had been so traumatised that it had been two years before she allowed Perry to have sex with her, but Perry was so understanding and had always been gentle and loving. He never once encouraged her to make contact with Grace, but said that he would come with her if she ever wanted to. Yet now even he was saying that it might be a good idea in the light of his situation and the fact that Grace was anxious to restore relations. The rape was horrific but Tiffany's feelings went back even further than that. She couldn't remember a period in her life when her sister hadn't been a bitch to her. An evil bitch! Could she ever forgive her?

'Do I need Grace's help?' Tiffany agonised. 'Do I need her back in my life?' It took her all of two seconds to come up with her answer.

'Success? You know what, I'm going to be a great success all on my own. I'm going to be the best mum in the whole wide world and I don't need anyone's help, especially not

Grace's, to achieve that. I wanted this baby. Giving birth to Chantelle was no accident: I could have had an abortion, but I didn't. I know exactly what I'm doing.' These were the triumphant words that Tiffany spoke to Linda on what was to be their last telephone conversation.

Tiffany worked hard. In an attempt to be the perfect mother she decided not to look for work for the moment. The best time for that would be when Chantelle was of school age, but that was some way off. Anyway, what could she do? Having left school at thirteen without taking her exams there weren't really a lot of options open to her. She weighed up her attributes: she was five foot ten, she could sing, she was slim, young and pretty. So jobwise she would have to be a singer or a model. Or maybe she'd have to wake up to the stark reality of life. The only thing she was realistically qualified to be was a cleaner. She might have seriously to consider that, or else go on some kind of training course. But all of this was something for the future. Right now, with Perry gone, there was only one thing for Tiffany to do and that was to give Chantelle the best educational start she could. That was what Chinella, her own mother, had done. By the time Tiffany and Grace were of school age they could both read and write and that was the very least Tiffany could do for her own child. No way was Chantelle going to end up like her. No way.

Tiffany showered her daughter with love and affection and as she did so she transformed herself from a little girl into a responsible young mother who ran a good home, keeping up payments of bills as well as monthly prison visits to Perry. A ten-year sentence was a long time but, with remission, he could be out in seven. She was ready and more than willing to wait.

9

Brixton Prison, 1978

Perry spent four months on remand. The first few weeks were in the cold comfort of police station cells from which he was taken back and forth to court.

In the eyes of the police Perry was scum, and they didn't try to hide the absolute contempt in which they held him. If the British justice system allowed them to go this far with him without any repercussions, what about his poor black brothers on the other side of the Atlantic or in South Africa? Had Perry lived and been caught in America's Deep South would he ever have been seen again?

He'd been caught in possession of stolen goods and had admitted robbing twenty-six homes in all, but now they were also trying to say that he ran some sort of house of prostitution, inviting men to have sex with the young boys they alleged he'd been brainwashing, and charging money for the privilege.

Tony, the boy who had taken the ring that led to Perry's arrest, had been easily persuaded to inform on everyone but it was one of the younger boys from the group who caused Perry's downfall. Tom had been asked by the police why he stayed with Perry. How was Perry able to make him do the unlawful things that they had all participated in? Was it money? Did Perry organise everything and give them money?

Tom thought for a while and then said, 'It was because of the sex, I suppose.'

'What do you mean when you say because of the sex, son? Explain that to us.'

'Well . . .' he began, very slowly and nervously. 'It all started when this man came around and told me that he'd give me some money, if I . . . if I, you know . . . played with him and let him play with me.' Tom looked up at their faces, hesitantly and slowly. He hadn't spoken about this to anyone but Perry. Was it something to be embarrassed about? How were they reacting? The policemen looked very considerate, giving him all their attention, and so he continued with a bit of added vigour. 'I ended up getting quite a bit of money in the end.'

'And it was Perry. Did Perry assist you in that area?'

'Yes, of course he did.'

'Now let's be very clear, are you saying that you were paid by a man to have sex with him?'

'Yes.'

The policemen huddled together for a while and as they parted one said, 'Men who do things like that to little boys aren't well. Men who do that type of thing have to be put away for a long time. Do you understand?'

'Yes.' Tom nodded.

'Well then, maybe you'll also understand that the person who allows that type of thing to go on is just as wrong, just as guilty. That person would be as guilty as the man who did that to you. Would you agree?'

'Yes,' whispered Tom.

'Well, Tom, you've got to tell us everything that happened to you, and in great detail so that we can put the bastards responsible away for a very, very long time. Do your parents know?'

'No way!' Tom flared.

Tom began to feel nervous again. He didn't want any fuss and he certainly didn't want his mum to find out. But what did sound attractive was the fact that the man would go to prison. He had never liked that man being all over him. And it had been a long time before the man left him alone. In fact it hadn't been until Perry intervened and came to his rescue.

'Don't be worried, Tom. Believe me, everything will be OK. Trust me.'

'That's exactly what Perry told me.'

One of the policemen couldn't contain himself. 'That black bastard,' he seethed as he punched at the air.

'I'm just a bit scared that he might come after me again and then I'd never be able to get away,' said Tom anxiously.

'You'll be fine, you really will, and just think, with your help, none of them will be able to put other little boys through what you've had to go through.'

'So he'd go down for a long time, then? And I would never see him again?'

'Yes. With your help, yes. Perry would never be able to get any other boys to do that again . . .'

At that moment the door to the interview room swung open and Perry was led in by a group of plain-clothed detectives.

'For God's sake!' yelled one of the policemen.

'Tom! Are you all right?' Perry asked with concern before being yanked out of the room again. Tom was left alone with one policeman as the others followed the detectives and Perry outside, closing the door behind them.

'It wasn't Perry that did it,' Tom told the remaining policeman. 'Perry was the one who stopped it,' he protested.

'It's all right, son. We'll take care of it from now on. There's no need for you to get scared again.'

The detectives were told of Tom's misguided revelations and decided to get the story out of Perry in whatever way they could. Perry was thrown into a cell and six officers followed him in.

They failed in their attempts to persuade Perry to admit to any sex charges. How could he agree to something he hadn't done? Subsequent interviews with Tom and the rest of the group also proved fruitless. But the police didn't believe them. They concluded that the boys were frightened of Perry and were protecting him. He'd become a kind of surrogate father to them all and now they felt beholden to him.

The police wouldn't let up on their investigation. They questioned neighbours who'd told them that there was always a string of men going in and out of the flat, but they needed more than just hearsay – they needed proof.

Perry accompanied them to his home, led in with his hands secured behind him in metal cuffs. Although they found nothing more, this visit deeply hurt Perry's pride. He felt that Tiffany should never have seen him in such a submissive state. Once he had had power, real power, but he realised that now he had been caught, how quickly that power had gone. And if he felt like this about himself, what did Tiffany think of him? He hung his head to disguise his feelings of shame as he was led around his home by two policemen.

'How old are you?' an arrogant WPC asked Tiffany with an indignant tone. Tiffany had stretched out her hand to give her yet another receipt slip and the policewoman caught hold of it and was scrutinising the two very expensive rings on her fingers.

'What's it to you?' Tiffany snapped with equal indignation as she snatched back her hand. 'I don't appreciate you doing that.'

'And I don't appreciate having to come to homes like yours because your boyfriend, and possibly you, decided not to work for a living. Where are the receipts for the rings that you're wearing?'

'Oh, for crying out loud! Do you want a receipt for the knickers I've got on too?'

'You don't realise how accommodating we're being. I could easily bag up everything in here and have it taken away for inspection.'

'Yeah? Who gives a fuck?'

'Right, take off the rings. If you want them back you'll have to come down to the station with proof of purchase.'

'Fuck off!'

'What did you say, you little black shit?'

Perry intervened quickly. He knew only too well how this could escalate.

'Tiffany, go get the receipts for the rings ... OK?' Tiffany stared at him. She was just about to tell him that he needed to stand up to these cheeky gits. She was just about to let him know that if he let them, they would walk all over him. She was just about to, but when she saw his face she stopped. Perry was dark in complexion but it was plain to see they had already walked all over him ... literally. His eyes were puffed up, his lip had been split open and there was a large bump on his forehead. She began to protest but he shook his head. It pained her deeply to see him like that, but mindful of his silent pleas she said nothing. It was a tough lesson in restraint, but she simply rose and went to find every receipt that remained. As she handed them to the policewoman, the tears that she had been trying so hard to keep inside trickled down her face. Tiffany angrily wiped them away and tried to ignore the smile of pleasure on the policewoman's lips.

They left ten minutes later, but this short visit had eaten away at Perry's ego, while strengthening Tiffany's resolve. Although she wanted the comforts that money brought, no way was she ever going to do anything illegal in order to get it. The police would never do to her what she could see they had done to Perry. No way.

Perry had never been without freedom before. He was moved from Shepherd's Bush police station to Wealdstone, before being sent to Brixton prison. Bail was constantly denied, his mother in America being cited as a possible incentive for him to try to leave the country. The police were also convinced that there was a large amount of stolen property still hidden somewhere and their subsequent enquiries would be thwarted if he were released. While his solicitor argued a good defence, aimed heavily at the heart-strings of a set of very pompous-looking magistrates, culminating in the fact that his young girlfriend was expecting their first baby and therefore he needed to be with her through the coming traumatic and emotional time, he was described by the prosecution as a very dangerous character who for many years had coerced younger boys into a life of crime.

He was further remanded in custody as the magistrates recommended that his case be heard in front of a Crown Court judge. They felt that the maximum sentence they could impose on him was woefully inadequate. On 17 August 1978, Perry Justice Walker was sentenced to ten years' imprisonment.

Perry felt it would take time to fit into his new environment and to begin with he asked Tiffany not to visit him. He would send her a visiting order as soon as he could, but for now he felt he needed to regain his composure without having to face her immediately. Perry had always been the leader of his merry group of impressionable boys, and he was finding it hard to adjust to being led. He didn't make friends easily and his pretty looks and tall, athletic frame attracted attention of a nature he didn't initially want, but which would ultimately change his whole attitude to sexuality.

There was a sense of expectancy in the air as a prisoner built like a gladiator, flanked by his two cronies, walked into the sparsely furnished prison recreation room. Paul, Dave and five others who were standing around the snooker table looked up at them and heeded an unspoken signal to leave, throwing their cues on to the table. One by one everyone left the room, except Perry, who didn't know the rules of this particular game.

Perry, who had been patiently waiting to play snooker, noticed one of Gordon the gladiator's cronies almost standing guard at the door. He tried not to think of the possible implications. What was he supposed to do? Get up and leave too? As Gordon walked towards him, Perry attempted to control the nervous twinges that gripped his stomach. One thing he knew he must not do was show any sign of fear.

'Anyone for a game?' he asked innocently.

That night he tried to shut out of his mind what followed, but the images kept recurring, forcing him to relive again and again the way his face had been smashed on to the pool table as he leaned forward to pick up one of the suspended wooden cues; the way a foam ball had been forced into his mouth, drowning out his cries for help; the way his struggles had proved fruitless once he realised what was about to take place; the way they'd ripped and forced his trousers down; the pain and the sheer helplessness that he felt when he experienced for the very first time a rigid penis penetrating his anal passage, and finally the smell of bad breath that Gordon had exhaled over Perry's face when he came.

They had left him lying there. He had crumpled

on to the floor of the recreation room, sobbing loudly, and when he eventually looked up he was sure he saw a prison warden look in, see him, and walk on by.

10

Kent, 1980

To anyone on the outside, four years of marriage had only improved the relationship between Clare and Peter Duvall. Clare's father had always made it clear that he was looking forward to having grandchildren and, although Peter was reluctant to start a family so early on in their marriage, Clare fell pregnant within a year.

Now they had three children: Jake, aged three, Thomas, two, and five-month-old Sarah, but as a result of Clare having the children so close together and Peter's change of career into politics, their marriage was facing mounting problems and pressures. Circumstances were leading them away from each other, to different destinations.

Being a housewife and mother to three children meant Clare had very little time for her husband and even less for herself. On top of everything she had never managed to get her figure back, especially after Sarah's birth, and now she was two stones heavier than when they married, and steadily gaining each day.

Her efforts to run their home smoothly and efficiently without any help – she refused to have staff because her mother never had and Clare had always wanted to be just like her mother – went unnoticed by Peter, who was having the busiest time of his life. The timing of his career move, the birth of their third child and preparations for moving house could not have been worse. In an attempt to cope and keep up the pretence of being a happy couple, they began to ignore what was happening between them. Even when, by some miracle, they managed to get to bed at the same time, Clare was always too exhausted even to contemplate making love. She brushed off Peter's advances by saying that she had a headache, felt sick or had to get up to feed Sarah. In reality, her sexual appetite had just seemed to die after Sarah was born: she wasn't at all interested and hoped Peter could see that, given the amount of work involved in looking after the children, her constant excuses of tiredness were justified. Peter did seem to accept it. Of late he hadn't pushed for them to make love any more so maybe he understood that she needed more time before things could get back to normal.

In fact, Peter was becoming more and more frustrated. He was finding it hard to adjust to no longer coming first in Clare's affections. Now he came fourth in the pecking order, after the children. His work in seeking the nomination to run for a safe seat in the House of Commons kept him very occupied, but not enough to obliterate his sexual desires. In fact Peter had always had a strong sex drive and in the first year of their marriage he had wanted to make love to Clare morning, noon and night. Now it had been three months since they last rolled between the sheets.

While she might not realise it, as a doctor, although specialising in cardiology, Peter was actually sympathetic to post-pregnancy problems and the fact that raging hormones sometimes caused extreme emotional upset. He could see that it was the children that had made Clare react the way she did to sex. Clare was his wife, she just needed some time and he would give her that, but if he couldn't have Clare's body, he at least wanted her mind. He was used to sharing everything with Clare, talking about his work, patients and politics, and in the past she had always been an intelligent listener, highlighting certain issues she had seen on the news and entering into long discussions. Now her conversation revolved around the difficulties that she was having removing stains from the children's clothing, whether to change washing powders, or the fact that Heinz had brought out a new flavour in their solid baby-food range. The gulf between them was steadily growing, but they knew that they still needed each other. Clare had to have a husband. They had three children and, although he might not offer anything other than financial help, she was married to this man and that was the way it was going to stay. Besides, the way she was feeling wasn't going to last forever.

Peter needed Clare for other reasons. His political career meant that he needed a wife and children simply for appearance's sake. He had to present the image that here was a man with strong family values. A Conservative MP without a family just wasn't on.

So the divide between them grew. They both knew that a problem existed, but neither of them mentioned it to each other, or did anything about it.

Peter didn't need any encouragement to stand for the selection committee. The opportunity came sooner than he had anticipated but he had always intended to go into politics full time in later life. His easy route to power came as a result of Clare's father pulling strings. The death of the former MP for Hazelhurst meant a by-election was due and, although Peter was bound to walk it, he still had to be seen to do a lot of groundwork. He made it his job to meet as many people from his prospective constituency as possible. He listened to their concerns, heard where their anger lay, understood what they wanted more of.

Clare didn't have time to get involved in the canvassing, the door-stepping, the meetings and rallies that Peter and his helpers had constantly to take part in. It was only after being selected to run for the safe Conservative seat that the real hard work began. It was work which kept Peter out till late at night and often forced him to leave home very early in the morning.

Clare could only applaud him from a distance most of the time. She felt that her children needed her much more than Peter did, surrounded as he was by his loyal team of workers. She didn't feel comfortable about what she was having to do, putting her children before her husband. She had wanted so much to follow in the footsteps of her mother, being the ever-giving and successful housewife, but she was falling well short of her ideals. Something had to give and it was her relationship with her husband that began to suffer.

The by-election came and Peter secured a seat in the House by a massive majority of 17,000. He had a great many interviews to do and then there were celebrations at the constituency office where Clare's father made sure that champagne flowed for all who had helped to secure the sweet victory. Clare went along for about half an hour and then left with her mother to take the children home, but Graham and Peter stayed. They had played equal parts in the handling of Peter's rise to power and now they had a right to share in the celebrations.

Sally Crimson had been Peter's right-hand woman long before the day Peter had to face the gruelling questions from the selection committee. Although his nomination was already secured thanks to Graham's contacts, Peter in his usual manner wanted to be geared up on every issue, especially local matters. But unlike the days when he prepared his political speeches at Cambridge, it wasn't Clare but Sally who stayed with him, sometimes late into the night, helping him to research and write letters, being his eyes and ears while he learned all that there was to know.

Because Sally was always there for him he came to trust her and soon started to share private matters with her, like the difficulties he was experiencing at home. Sally was always very sympathetic. She always seemed to have the answer to his dilemmas.

It was near to midnight when Graham asked for a car to be ordered to take him home. Peter decided that he was due a real night of celebrations. It would be, he believed, his last night of fun for a very long time and he wanted to make the best of it. He declined Graham's invitation to share his car.

'I'm proud of you, son. You know that, don't you? You know, I've only got one girl, Clare's my baby and always will be. You know how much I love her and I'll do anything for her, but you, Peter, I see you as my son. That's why I will always do my best to help you. Congratulations again, son.' He slapped Peter hard on the back before putting his cigar in the side of his mouth and climbing into the waiting taxi. From the back seat, Graham wound down the window and Peter leaned forward in order to continue their conversation.

'Graham? I can't thank you enough. I hope you know how grateful I am to you for . . . for everything, but . . . I've always wondered. Why did you never want to stand yourself? I mean, you know everyone, from the PM down, but apart from supporting them and being a member of the party, you've never talked about running for parliament. I've always found that strange.'

'It just hasn't interested me and, quite frankly, some of us are destined for different things. And could you imagine what Mary would say if I was out of the house even more than I am now? Being an MP is going to keep you very busy, my son, very busy.'

'Oh, I think I've already had a taste of how busy I'm going to be.'

'Well, mark my words, it will get much worse. But it will be worth it.'

Peter was still reflecting on Graham's words when Sally tapped him on the shoulder.

'There you are. I've been looking all over for you.' She noticed his expression. 'What's wrong?'

'Graham just left. I just came out here to see him off.'

'Yes? And? What did he say? When I spoke to him earlier he seemed as over the moon as you did, but what's wrong with you now?'

'It's not that anything's wrong as such.'

'Come on, Peter. This is Sally, remember? I know you. I know that there's a problem.'

'It's just that all of this, Sally, is really down to Graham. I mean, without him, would any of this have been possible?'

'Of course it would! I don't think that you took any short cuts. I was with you, remember? I was with you all the way and it was your hard work that won this election, not Graham.'

'Oh, come on, Sally. I know what the reality is. It's just like when I left Cambridge, zoom, just like that I become a junior partner in a top Harley Street practice. And now, just four years later, I'm the bloody MP for Hazelhurst. You and I know that this is all down to him.'

'Look, if you're saying that Graham made things happen more quickly for you than they would have done if you weren't married to his daughter, then yes, maybe that is the case, but you weren't complacent: you worked bloody hard and you deserve every single bit of the success.' Sally reached for his hand. Holding it gently as she raised it to her lips, she said, 'Don't ever forget that none of this would have been possible without you. Without *you*, not Graham.' Sally kissed his knuckles a few times.

Good old Sally, always there to snap him out of any negative moods. Always there as a shoulder to cry on.

'Hey! I haven't even given you a hug yet and said thank you for everything that you've done for me.' Peter released his hand from hers, wrapped his arms around her and rested his cheek on the side of her face. 'Thank you,' he gently whispered in her ear.

Sally giggled. 'You have said thank you, many, many times, and it really has been my pleasure. Really.' She brought her head round to face him. As she did so, their lips brushed and he allowed himself a friendly peck, but it meant more to both of them than just that. As he looked at her he knew what he wanted. But what about Clare, should he be feeling like this? If he allowed it to happen, what would he be getting into? Did he want Sally for her own sake or because he hadn't had sex with his wife for so long? Or was it just the booze making him feel overly frisky? When he finally plucked up the courage to kiss Sally it wasn't just a friendly kiss.

This time it was the kiss that started his first extra-marital affair.

11

Islington,
1982

Marcia Abiola wondered if Cyril Ridney had washed that morning. As she kneeled down in front of him, crouching between his spread-eagled legs, his dick tasted very salty. She'd have to make him come very quickly so that she could go and wash out her mouth and reapply her lipstick.

Cyril Ridney had been editor on the *Islington Tribune* for thirteen years. He was a forty-two-year-old Caucasian, young in appearance, dark haired and good-looking, but never before had he found himself in such a fortunate position.

Marcia had intially come to the paper straight from school where her form teacher had recommended that she follow up her instinctive talents. She'd done well in her exams and at sixteen Marcia was a bright, bubbly girl with an eye for a story and flair and originality as a writer. At her interview she'd made it clear that college was not for her. She wanted to get straight into the working environment and gain crucial on-the-job experience.

Cyril Ridney had set her a piece to write, along with twenty-one other applicants for the post of junior reporter on his paper – except that they had all been to college. But when he saw Marcia's work he had no doubt that she was the best and had something special to offer. He encouraged her to work for him over the summer holidays and meanwhile to apply for a three-year course in media studies to broaden her natural talent. When the college received his written recommendation, she was accepted.

Her summer holidays during the course were spent working for the *Islington Tribune* and, on qualifying, Cyril gave her a full-time job as a reporter. That was a year ago and today was the first time that an employee had given him such a welcome – and totally unsolicited – sexual favour.

Unlike the other juniors, Marcia was always enthusiastic and her love for her work really showed. Often she would work late into the evening. Tapping away with nimble fingers, she typed up her copy from the scribbles in her note pad which formed the exclusive shorthand that only she could decipher.

Even though Marcia sometimes worked as late as nine o'clock in the evening, she never left before Cyril. There was always lots of movement in his office; the phone rang, she could hear him having conversations and laughing, but on this particular evening there was a noticeable, almost uncomfortable silence. Marcia was used to being the only one in the main office late at night, but what had happened to Cyril that evening? The silence unnerved her, distracting her from the story she was writing about some teenagers who were going around Islington impersonating charity collectors and had so far swindled old folk out of nearly £1,000. What was wrong with him? After ten minutes she realised she would have to find out.

He was slumped across his desk with his head in his arms when she walked in. He looked up, startled, and jumped to his feet.

'Oh, Marcia? It's you. God, I really don't want you to see me like this.'

She wanted to tell him that she wasn't exactly thrilled to be dragged away from her work by his silence to find out what was wrong with him. She wanted to say that, but she didn't. She still needed a job.

'Is everything all right?' she asked, summoning up an appropriate tone of concern.

Cyril didn't need to be asked twice. The past seven months had been a nightmare and there was nothing that he could do about it. His only method of coping had been to stay away from home as much as possible.

'She's dying, my wife is dying and there's nothing that I, or anyone else, can do about it. She's got breast cancer. I know that I should be there with her. I should be by her side right now, holding her hand, giving her support, comforting her, but I just can't. She's not the woman I married, and if I'm really honest with myself . . . what I feel for her isn't love any more. It's, it's . . . I feel anger and pity and . . . and guilt. Yes, guilt, because I know that these aren't the feelings that I should be having. Staying in this office night after night while her mother does the job that I should be doing, staying in this office so that when I get home she's already asleep and I don't have to . . . I know that I shouldn't be doing it, I know that it's wrong, but I can't help it. I can't bring myself to do the right thing any more. I've had as much as I can take. Do you understand, Marcia? Do you?'

Strangely enough, she did. She couldn't think of anything worse than having to look after someone who was ill and totally dependent on her. Her mother was now a trapped spirit having finally married one of her many lovers, and thank God for that, because in her mother's old age Marcia was the last person who would be prepared to fetch and carry a bedpan for her. Oh no! She looked at Cyril Ridney, leaning against the desk, his arms folded, his head bent, his eyes shut. She couldn't feel any sympathy. Her natural make-up didn't allow for that type of sentimentality. She'd heard his story and basically wanted to get back to her own.

Except there was another idea beginning to take shape in her head. For the first time she had the upper hand over her boss. He had confided in her, admitted his shortcomings. There must be some way she could take advantage.

In the office earlier that day a group of reporters had been discussing a training course they had read about which was taking place at the Islington Tec. It was a crash course on media communication lasting only twelve weeks. The big attraction for Marcia was that it dealt with some areas of television. Television, they all knew, was something that was going to grow and grow. It was the medium that Marcia could ultimately see herself working in and she didn't want to miss this opportunity, but they were all in the same boat. None of them was earning enough to afford it. Someone suggested that they approach Mr Ridney because surely, if he paid for some of them to go on the course, he'd have a more informed team of journalists. They all laughed and told the person who made the suggestion to wake up. Mr Ridney was a good boss on many levels, but his charity did not extend to eating into the profits of the paper. He had shown himself to be a very tough negotiator and anyway, how was a course that concentrated largely on television journalism going to benefit him?

Marcia wanted to do it. She had made up her mind, despite the fact that it would cost too much and she couldn't afford to take the time off work. It was imperative for her career that she go on the course. Now maybe she had a chance. If she scratched Cyril's back (or front), maybe he would do something for her? Of course she didn't want a favour for nothing, but maybe they could work something out.

As for Cyril, all he wanted was a shoulder to cry on,

someone to listen to him. Who better than Marcia? She was a good journalist. She'd been able to dig up the most amazing information on people and her interviews were always full of interesting detail. That must mean she was a good listener. But while Marcia might have heard all Cyril's problems, all they amounted to in her eyes was one thing: sexual frustration. Her mother's tirades about weak men echoed in her ears. The man before her had not had sex for a long time and that meant he was weak and most probably vulnerable.

She walked over and held him in her arms. She began to run her fingers through his hair and blow softly in his ear. When he realised that he was being seduced as opposed to comforted, he grabbed Marcia's arms from around his body and pushed her back. Their eyes met. She knew she looked great and she knew that he was seeing it for the first time. At twenty, following in her mother's footsteps, Marcia took great care of her physical appearance. She was a very attractive, full-figured, intelligent woman who had had her first date at fourteen, lost her virginity at fifteen (by choice) and was currently seeing three different men. She dictated the terms of her relationships and if anyone ever complained, she got rid of them. It was her life and she lived it the way she wanted.

This was no time for Cyril to think about his wife. He would have to put her totally out of his mind, because he was a man and he needed to have a sexual release. It was his natural right. He pulled her against him. Their lips touched lightly, again and again, and then harder. Their tongues met and entwined. Marcia began to massage him through his trousers. He was panting heavily as she undid the zip. And when she put his dick in her mouth, he held her head to it.

Once she had washed out her mouth and reapplied her lipstick, Marcia returned to Cyril's office and neatly led the conversation round to the course and how much she wanted to attend it and the fact that she couldn't afford the £150 entrance fee. Cyril Ridney had his back to her and when he turned round Marcia was amazed by his words. She hadn't reckoned with the reaction of a guilt-ridden man who knew he had done wrong and wasn't about to be compromised any further.

'You're fired! Yes, you heard me!' He squashed her suggestion like a newspaper on a fly. 'You thought that if you had sex with me I would turn round and keep you like a mistress?'

'No. I just thought that . . .'

'Well you thought fucking wrong then, didn't you? Or maybe I should say you didn't think at all. I'm not giving you £150, I'm not even going to give you £15. The only thing that you're going to get from me now is your P45. You're fired!'

Marcia sat at her kitchen table and raised the envelope to her lips, licking the seal. She placed the envelope on her dining-room table ready for posting and patted it. This was something to be proud of; she was a journalist, after all, and if that didn't give her some kind of dramatic licence what profession would? She'd had to do it anyway. Cyril Ridney was not going to get away with it. He had pushed her to it, but she wasn't bothered about her lack of employment. It was just another lesson to be learned in life's sweet path. She now knew that if she was ever in that situation again, whatever she wanted out of it had to be negotiated first. It made no sense bargaining after the event. As for Cyril Ridney, he'd hurt her feelings and her pride and someone had to pay. She'd exaggerated their brief liaison in the letter, but did a wife who was dying of cancer really care whether her husband had been unfaithful once or fifty times? The mere knowledge that he had, in her time of pain and suffering, done it at all would surely be devastating enough. As she opened the local paper and looked down the 'Situations Vacant' columns, Marcia noticed an ad for a journalist to join the popular paper aimed at the Afro-Caribbean community, *Your Choice*. Well, at least she had already seen the possibility of a future for herself.

She wondered idly how her letter would affect the future of Mrs Cyril Ridney.

12

Lowestoft Open Prison, 1980-83

To Perry's great relief there was a positive response to his first application to transfer to an open prison and as he soon found out, you could get anything into Lowestoft.

Set about a mile back from the main road, it was enclosed by fields and gardens looked after by the prisoners who took great pride in their horticultural work. Perry was transferred there after just two years in Brixton, where he had swallowed any pride that he had left and learned what he had to do, and what he had to become, in order to survive. He wasn't tough enough to be a 'bad boy'. Although he might have been involved in criminal activities, he wasn't a real hardened criminal and was well out of his depth in Brixton. Unlike most of the inmates, he didn't know anyone there. His gang of boys were too young to be tried at the same level as him. Three of them received youth custodial sentences of six months. The twelve- and thirteen-year-olds were too young even for that, although Tom was eventually taken into care.

As a result of what he had witnessed and experienced in Brixton, Perry was scared of the consequences of being without 'friends' or back-up in prison, though he never shared his fears with Tiffany who had begun to visit him on a monthly basis. But she noticed a definite change in his attitude. He had become coarse and seemed to have lost any real signs of tenderness and emotion. The only time they touched each other was when Tiffany arrived and left. Then they would kiss, but if during the visit Tiffany stretched her hand across the table to take his, she could sense that it made him uncomfortable.

He never told her about his experience with Gordon. Since that first incident there had been others which had all served to transform Perry into the changed man he had become. Within a few weeks at Brixton he'd seen more than a few fights and almost been involved in a couple himself. He vividly remembered the time he was taking a shower with six other inmates. Almost casually a prisoner, whom he later learned was serving twenty-five years for murdering a policeman and armed robbery, walked into the shower room fully clothed, took out something which had been strapped to his calf and proceeded to run whatever it was across the throat of the man showering beside him. Perry very quickly realised that that 'something' was a sliver of glass and as the victim clasped at his throat before falling back against the wall, making throttling sounds and gasping for air, a gush of blood splashed on to his body. Mixing with the clear water, it made its way down his torso and flowed towards the drains over and around Perry's feet. Before leaving, the assailant gave Perry a look which meant, 'if you talk, you'll follow'. Perry also found out later that the victim had lost his life for an overdue debt of money and cigarettes. Perry was no fool; he didn't deny he was scared.

While gay men were despised in that environment, being in prison for a long time made even the straightest of men contemplate the unthinkable. And having a wank didn't always suffice. Although Gordon was gay, his size meant that not many men looked in his direction, much less troubled him. His six-foot-five stature also guaranteed a form of asylum for any of his followers.

You couldn't be left alone when you looked like Perry. He was under constant threat. He could either be bullied by the tougher guys who, if crossed, would not think twice about trying to end his existence, or he could become a 'friend' of Gordon. It didn't take long for him to decide which way to go. After all, his initial ordeal with Gordon had left him hurt but alive; the man in the shower was very much dead. Perry derived a feeling of safety from Gordon's company but he had to pay for that protection with sexual favours. How ironic all of this was. In his earlier life he would have tried to kill a man for doing exactly the same thing, and nearly did in Tom's case. Here in prison he had become exactly what he once despised.

Now he had left Gordon and his cronies behind, Perry found Lowestoft very easy-going. He spent most of his time playing chess and backgammon, which he'd learned to master in Brixton.

Tiffany kept up her monthly visits but not because she wanted to any more. When Perry first went down she had always looked forward to seeing him and would take Chantelle, treasuring the comparatively short visiting times that they spent together Now she hated them. He just would not explain the change in him and what was particularly scary for Tiffany was his total denial that any change had taken place. Could he really not see or feel it? That possibility frightened Tiffany, and so did his new request.

Before he'd never wanted Tiffany to get directly involved in anything that was illegal or dangerous but now it was different. Now she was to become his delivery service. Now things had changed so much between them that he didn't mind her being at risk. And now she only visited out of a sense of duty and had even stopped taking

Chantelle, not that Perry appeared to have noticed. He was too busy trying to convince her to take part in his latest development at Lowestoft.

She wouldn't agree to it at first but his constant reminders of what she owed him wore her down. For more than three years he had given her a home, love, support and happiness. He'd shared everything with her and given her the security she had always wanted, but now, when he needed her, she was turning her back on him. This wasn't the way that Tiffany wanted to repay him for all that he had done for her. She did want him to need her but not in the way that he wanted to use her. She had become just a ticket: a meal ticket, a cigarette ticket, a food ticket. Where had all their love gone? 'You owe me,' he informed her on countless occasions.

'But didn't you look after me out of love and concern . . . ? Anyway, why don't you ask one of the boys to do it? I can easily get a message to one of them. All you have to do is send them next month's visiting order.'

'They could be searched, so there's a risk. I want you to do it.'

'Yeah, and what if they search me? What if I get caught? What about Chantelle?'

'They won't search you. You owe me, Tiff. I gave you everything. I gave you security. I gave you everything and took nothing from you in return.'

It was dawning on her that there was always a price to pay, but this time he wouldn't be the only one paying it if things went wrong. There would be deeper repercussions affecting her and, more importantly, Chantelle. And she'd vowed never to do *anything* illegal. But what did he care? He even wanted her to use the money in her building society account, money he knew that she had been saving, money which had been accumulating interest for his return.

It was Sunday afternoon and the first day of their new arrangement. Tiffany was going to be visiting soon and he couldn't wait. As long as she did what he told her everything would be fine, and he would have found a way to command some respect within the system.

They met and embraced and, sure enough, when she kissed him they exchanged a tightly compressed package which Perry kept in his mouth for the duration of the visit. Its contents would make him a very popular inmate.

When Tiffany left that afternoon, she was very aware of the large notice that warned of the consequences of being caught bringing drugs into the prison.

13

Ealing, October 1983

Tiffany read the letter over and over and deliberated about contacting her sister. Again, it had been forwarded to her from social services and again it begged for a reunion. It concluded:

'. . . and I recently had an accident which means that I can't go to work for at least the next eight weeks. I've had a lot of time to reflect on the relationship that we had when we were young, time to reflect on the things that I did to you, and what I allowed to be done to you. While I can't alter the past, I want to make amends and look to the future. I know you are aware that I've tried to contact you many times. Please, I am asking for your forgiveness. I know that it may be hard for you to forget, but please find it in your heart to forgive me. I have been told that you have a little girl and I would very much like the opportunity to become part of your family again. You are all the family I've got. Please forgive me and contact me soon.'

Unlike the previous letters, Tiffany didn't throw it away. She still thought about Grace at some point every day. But while it didn't hurt as much any more she still didn't feel ready. Right now, with what Perry was putting her through, she didn't need any additional pressure.

Given the time that mother and daughter spent alone working together, it was no surprise that Chantelle was reading by the age of three and could even write her name. Tiffany used this to gain a place for her daughter at a state-subsidised nursery school. Preferring to keep herself to herself, she had never forged any friendships with other mothers living in her block of flats so it was new for Chantelle to start socialising all day with children of her own age. Initially it was fun and she enjoyed it, but she had to get used to a whole new process of learning and sharing.

Tiffany had kept up the visits to Lowestoft but nearly two years had elapsed since she had last taken Chantelle to see her father. Yet apart from the odd question about her achievements, Perry didn't seem to mind. His attitude hadn't changed and Tiffany was beginning to question why she constantly subjected herself to the possibility of her child being taken away from her, not to mention a six-month prison sentence if she was caught taking in drugs. And the account that she was using to buy the drugs was steadily running out.

Tiffany decided she needed to give herself a treat, do something for herself for a change. She decided to learn to drive and so one Thursday morning in October she found herself walking down her local high street to withdraw the cash she needed for her first lessons from her ever-diminishing funds. The High Street was the same as usual, busy and impersonal, but it harboured a surprise for Tiffany. Among the many familiar and unfamiliar faces that she passed was that of a photographer from her local paper who once a month stalked the High Street taking photographs of people – anybody, fat, thin, tall, short, black or white. The only criterion was that they must not be looking at him while he was discreetly snapping away. He noticed Tiffany and took a photograph of her for a monthly competition that the paper ran called 'Face of Fortune'. It was run for fun and as an incentive for locals to buy the paper; it had nothing to do with the way you looked, but there was a grand prize of £500.

Tiffany learned the news that she had won that month's competition from her caretaker. As she was returning from dropping Chantelle off at the nursery one morning a few days later, he rushed into his downstairs office and retrieved a copy of that morning's *Ealing Chronicle*.

'Oh . . . wow.' Tiffany was thrilled. She was always short of money these days and this was certainly going to come in handy. She could hardly contain her excitement as she went into her bedroom to change. She had to wear the same clothes she had been wearing in the photograph as identification when she went to the *Chronicle*'s offices to claim her prize. She wanted to wear her expensive rings as this was a special occasion and she went to fetch them from her bedroom drawer. It was then that she found Grace's letter and re-read it.

'Why not?' she thought. 'I'll never be in a more accommodating mood than I am today. Well, here goes,' she said to herself as she sat down beside the phone.

'We always do a short piece on what the winner is going to spend the money on. Have you thought about that yet, Tiffany?' asked the eager young reporter from the *Chronicle*, who was pleasantly surprised to see that the photographer had snapped someone attractive for a change. '. . . And please don't say that you're going to pay your bills,' he joked. 'They all say that.'

But that was exactly what she *had* envisaged doing with the money, and she had a choice of which one should take priority – gas, electricity or phone bill? She searched for something original to tell him and then she remembered the career alternatives that she'd very lightly contemplated a few years back. While she had no intention of paying anything other than those wretched bills initially, what she came up with wasn't really a a lie. If there was something left over she could make a start in that direction, especially since Chantelle had just started primary school.

'I've been thinking about becoming a model,' she confessed. 'So I think that I'll put it towards the cost of a portfolio.'

'Ah, you want to be a model? Hold on a minute.'

In less than a minute he was back with the news that the editor had agreed to his idea that they should run a full story on her accompanied by a photograph. They'd call her shortly to set up a session.

The following week the front-page headline read:

TIFFANY MODELS A FASHIONABLE CAREER

TIFFANY IDEH left school at the tender age of 13 and, even so, toyed with the idea of becoming an accountant. But now the 21-year-old South Ealing beauty is interested in figures of a different kind.

Tiffany is hoping that her stunning 35–24–35 figure will help to launch her into a modelling career.

She is now looking for a way to make the break from her flat on the South Ealing Estate into the world of glamour.

Tiffany says, 'I really want to be the black Jerry Hall – a top fashion model.'

The copy was underneath a large photograph of Tiffany.

'Look at that, Chantelle, front-page headlines,' Tiffany said proudly to her daughter as the doorbell rang. 'Whatever next?'

14

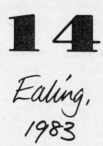

Ealing,
1983

Everything seemed to be happening so quickly. Grace was so thrilled to hear from Tiffany again that she came right over that same evening.

Tiffany studied her sister carefully as Grace talked non-stop and concluded that she hadn't really changed. Everything she had been before had just . . . grown. She had put on a lot of weight and now she was probably up to a size twenty but, even so, Grace was really articulate and had a bubbly personality. Tiffany liked what she saw and heard and regretted her decision to let so much time pass without getting in touch.

Grace, on the other hand, could see enormous changes in Tiffany. Everything was not just bigger but better, even her height. At least in the old days Grace had been taller than Tiffany. Now she didn't even have that. And then of course she was also less than half Grace's weight.

There was so much to catch up on it took them until the early hours of the morning to cover everything. In the years since her hasty exit from British Airways Grace had given up looking for another job, disillusioned by the countless rejections she'd received. To drown her disappointment and boredom she had taken to drink and, during this first meeting with her sister, she downed most of the bottle of Scotch she had brought with her. The alcohol tasted great and helped to moderate her down moods by altering her natural mental state. She knew that she was becoming addicted and had hoped that at least drink might have been something she could share with Tiffany. There was nothing more lonely than having to drink alone. But Grace was disappointed to find that Tiffany didn't touch the stuff and never had. Not that that stopped Grace. It gave her comfort, she explained to Tiffany.

Evidently not enough. It wasn't giving her the sort of ease that Tiffany obviously derived from life. As Grace looked around Tiffany's plush home, she was envious of what her sister had been able to achieve.

Over the next few weeks the sisters began to see a good deal of each other. Grace lied to Tiffany about her success at work and about how all her bosses had fancied her. Tiffany, never realising she wasn't being told the truth, felt genuinely pleased that she had taken the plunge and dialled her sister's number. Of course she had Chantelle, but she'd missed having an adult to talk to, someone to laugh with, someone who knew her past, someone to share things with. And that's exactly what she did. Over the next few weeks, Grace discovered everything that there was to know about Tiffany and Chantelle. Tiffany even confided in her about Perry and how any feelings that she'd had for him had now died. She told Grace all about how they'd met, how he had changed and about his activities, outside and now in prison.

Grace pretended to be horrified at Tiffany's involvement with someone who seemed so irresponsible. The most important person right now, she told Tiffany, was Chantelle. 'Chantelle is a child. An innocent party. You can't allow yourself to get drawn into anything illegal that may have repercussions on her life. Your daughter's welfare should be paramount. What could Perry possibly offer after his release but a training course into the criminal fraternity for Chantelle? Is that really what you want for your daughter?'

Tiffany didn't need much persuading. Grace convinced her not only to stop taking drugs into the prison for Perry but that it was best for all concerned to end their relationship. Grace dictated a Dear John letter for her to send to Perry. When Grace was dictating a line which seemed particularly cruel and Tiffany began to show signs of weakening, Grace said, 'Look, no man could love a woman and tell her to do that. You took illegal substances into the prison and what would have happened if you'd got caught? Do you really think that he cared? He may have helped you in the past but that was because you thought that you needed him and had no-one else. But I'm here now. You've got me to share things with.'

She seemed so comforting. Unfortunately she didn't mean a word of it and while Tiffany poured out her heart to Grace, Grace never revealed anything about her own miserable life.

Grace had another agenda. Since her sacking, the feelings that Grace had for Tiffany had festered and deteriorated even further. She was out to wreak revenge on Tiffany for everything she'd had to put up with as a result of her being born. All the old resentment about her parents, Uncle Kema and Kevin resurfaced. Tiffany had made a success of her life. She had everything: beauty, work, a child, a lovely home.

Grace began to make a deliberate attempt to find out anything that was negative about Tiffany. She wasn't quite sure how she was going to engineer her downfall but she was determined to gather as much information as possible to use against her sister in the future.

She noticed, for instance, that although Chantelle was

very dear to Tiffany, Tiffany sometimes tried to hide her existence. Grace wondered why.

'There's one thing that I want to ask you,' she probed one day. 'That article that you gave me to read about you in the *Ealing Chronicle*, I noticed that it didn't mention Chantelle.'

'That was deliberate. I didn't know whether it was a good or a bad thing to have a child and say that I was trying to get into modelling. I didn't know if it would have put off any interested parties.'

'Oh,' Grace nodded, 'of course,' and filed away the information for further use.

An agent had called Tiffany as a result of seeing the article in the *Chronicle* and now Tiffany was being professionally represented by Top Ones, a leading model agency. She'd been thrown right in at the deep end. The first taste of her new life came when she was sent along to an audition for a fashion show at Bruce Oldfield's in Beauchamp Place, to find models to launch his latest Autumn/Winter collection.

She'd envisaged being asked to walk up and down a showroom in front of a host of beady eyes, who would call out '*next*' if she didn't meet their requirements. In order to prepare, she cleared an aisle between the furniture in her sitting room and practised walking to music for a whole evening under instruction from Grace and Chantelle. But when she got to the audition all that she had to do was try on some clothes. Everything fitted and looked wonderful on her, and she landed the job.

She was fortunate to have started at the beginning of the fashion season and soon she was working regularly for many top British designers including Bruce Oldfield, Zandra Rhodes and Caroline Charles.

Although only a tiny number make it in the cut-throat world of modelling, Tiffany's striking good looks, her fine cheekbones and long, long legs struck a chord, and she quickly found herself in demand. Clothes simply looked great on her, and her naturally patient nature made it easy for her to cope with the hours spent sitting around at castings and the exhausting demands of photographers.

Grace had invented a fictitious injury to explain the reason she was off work. Tiffany offered sympathy but she never enquired as to the exact nature of Grace's ailment. She was just glad that her time off work was so well timed. It meant that Grace was available to collect Chantelle from school, as well as feed her and stay with her until Tiffany got back from work.

As days and weeks passed under this new arrangement, Tiffany's maternal instincts cried out to her. She often expressed her guilt to Grace about the lack of time that she was spending with Chantelle. She was also aware of how much she owed Grace for looking after her niece.

'Believe me, it's no imposition,' Grace told Tiffany. 'I really enjoy it and as for Chantelle, really, she doesn't even notice you're not there. By the way, have you told the agency that you've got a child?'

'No. I know I ought to but it's better they don't know quite yet. They'll just get the impression that I won't be able to work if anything comes up. I will tell them, when I've got my foot in the door, but not yet.'

'Oh, I understand – and don't you ever feel guilty. If you don't work, how are you going to pay the bills or buy the nice things that you're always buying for Chantelle?'

It was Grace herself who volunteered to move in and look after Chantelle when Tiffany was offered a modelling shoot in the Seychelles. It went so well that she was offered more and more work abroad and Grace cheerfully pretended the doctor had advised her to give up work for a while. Six months later Grace was still living with Tiffany. What was more she had every intention of staying there and expanding her role as Chantelle's surrogate mother.

Grace moved all of her belongings from Brixton to Ealing

but she didn't want Tiffany to feel that she was going to take over or move in forever. She made it clear that she still had her Brixton flat, even gave Tiffany a set of spare keys – 'Just in case you ever want to go there for a bit of peace and quiet!' – knowing Tiffany would never go near the place. She had to let Tiffany believe that she had sacrificed her pay packet and home for her. The reality was that Grace's flat wasn't homely and looked nothing like Tiffany's. In comparison, living with Tiffany was sheer luxury, and why not stay close to where she was hoping to wreak havoc?

All of her savings had been used up and she'd just applied for Social Security. If her claim was successful it would be the Social that would pay her rent on the Brixton flat, so she wouldn't be losing out financially by having two places to live. At Tiffany's she didn't have to pay a penny, but Tiffany didn't mind and wasn't suspicious that Grace was doing anything untoward. All that Grace's presence meant was that Tiffany had what she thought was her best friend to talk to and a live-in babysitter. Tiffany was earning enough money for all of them to live on and, really, she didn't have any other option.

It wasn't long before Grace, through her manipulations, had almost taken over as Chantelle's mother. Tiffany was relying on her as a sister, friend, confidante and nanny, and to Chantelle Grace was becoming the person who was always there for her, the one who cared. It was even Grace who met the teachers and went along to parents' evenings at Chantelle's school.

Chantelle was growing to love Grace and she began to confide in her aunt. She told her that she felt she never saw her mother these days. She thought that her mother didn't seem to have any time for her.

'Doesn't she love me any more?' she would ask constantly, and Grace would give her a reassuring hug and tell her with a smile, 'I'm afraid it looks as though your mum only loves herself and ... do you know, sometimes she doesn't even tell people she has a little girl. But don't worry. I love you, I'll look after you. OK, darling?'

Grace would always be careful to make it sound as if it were their private joke about Tiffany but she knew that little by little Chantelle was beginning to believe her mother didn't love her. Now, every time she said, 'OK, darling?' to Chantelle, Chantelle always came back with a smile, 'OK, Aunty Grace.'

But it wasn't OK. Chantelle had started at Ealing Primary School before her fifth birthday, impressing her teacher and head so much that they decided she should be educated with the five- and six-year-olds. But now, four months into the new arrangement, where Grace was everything to her while simultaneously feeding her inaccurate, hurtful information, Chantelle began to get into trouble at school. She started bullying other children, being rude to teachers and not taking any interest in her lessons. The teachers sent letters asking to see Tiffany but Grace intercepted them and told the school that Tiffany was too busy to attend and that she had taken over as legal guardian. Because Grace was the only person they had seen of late taking any interest in Chantelle's education, they had no reason to doubt her words. Between them, Grace and the teachers tried to work through the initial problems by giving Chantelle extra help and attention, but things just grew progressively worse. The decision was made to put her back in a class with children of the same age as herself. What was so hard for her teachers to understand was the complete change in Chantelle, her sudden eagerness to be naughty and to get caught. It was as though she was seeking attention, and any kind would do. Her vocabulary, helped by her close contact with Grace, and her mind were those of a child much older than her years. But she had also become very cynical and seemed to trust and respect no-one except Grace.

And Tiffany, constantly away on modelling assignments, knew nothing of her daughter's problems.

Perry wrote to Tiffany frequently. With all that he was having to face, how could she possibly leave him now? He also pointed out that he had only eighteen months of his sentence left to serve and that when he came back, things would be back to normal. He even said there was no need to bring him 'parcels' any more, he just wanted to see her.

She'd replied to his first letter reiterating her decision and refusing to go to see him. She might have responded to the other letters that he sent in the same way if she'd ever seen them. Grace always intercepted the post and kept Perry's letters and visiting orders away from Tiffany. She didn't throw them away.

She never threw anything away. She never knew when she might need it.

15

Islington,
1984

The editor of *Your Choice* smiled at Marcia, who was eager to hear his comments. It was her first major article and he'd put a lot of trust in her by asking her to write their lead feature for the following week. Tension was building across London between two racial groups. There had been countless incidents of indiscriminate beatings and murders. *Your Choice* wanted to run an article to reflect the mood of its readers. It read:

> PICTURE this. A young, happy-go-lucky, law-abiding male is on his way home. His mind is on his girlfriend, his exam results, Arsenal's away win the day before. It's dark outside, but it's not that late; besides, he's in an area he knows and he hasn't done anything wrong, so he isn't unduly concerned. Suddenly, his peaceful walk is interrupted. Suddenly, his mind is full of fear. Suddenly, his only concern is to run for his life.

Stephen Taylor, Kurdass Sahli, Marshall Temper

were all brutally attacked and two were murdered, simply because of the colour of their skins. Their names must be added to the list of forty previous killings: mothers left without their sons; sisters left without brothers; every decent living citizen, regardless of colour, left feeling sick and angry.

Again, picture this. Paul Smith applies for a position as a City clerk. His application is neatly presented and his CV shows that he has all the right qualifications and experience. His name is placed on a shortlist and he is contacted by phone regarding an interview. Written notes are taken of the ensuing conversation and the interviewer praises his personality and clear diction. He seems like the ideal candidate ... but unfortunately Paul Smith doesn't get the job. It transpires that Paul Smith, with an English name and English accent, isn't quite what they are looking for after all. He isn't quite what they thought he was. On paper he was great, on the telephone too, but Paul Smith on interview day was black.

Dressed smartly, on her way to work, Doreen McFarlane stops off at Tulip Fashions to buy a present for a colleague. She walks from rail to rail, from display to display. She can't quite make up her mind about what she wants to buy. She has every right to take her time yet she begins to feel uncomfortable because she catches the security guard keeping a close eye on her every move. She ignores him, selects her garment and joins the queue at the cash desk. Suddenly the old woman in front of Doreen McFarlane becomes nervous. She starts to protect her handbag as if she is afraid someone behind her is going to steal something from it. Because the someone behind her is black.

This is not paranoia. Like an ever-burning

Olympic torch, the flames of racism constantly flare and, day in, day out, black people have to put up with situations that their white counterparts would find intolerable.

Regardless of geography, the message has always been that if you're white you're all right, if you're black step back, and for many years they did. The majority of the steady flow of black people who came to Britain through the forties, fifties and sixties didn't want to rock the boat. They wanted to fit in, they just wanted a peaceful life and, after all, they were here by invitation. But now, first- and second-generation blacks are demanding equal rights and opportunities. Having helped build the country into what it is today, black people demand fairness.

The ratio of black people to white in British prisons is totally out of proportion to the number of black people in the country. Is the judiciary trying to detain as many as possible because society would be a better place without them or because it makes him feel safe? All that is being created in this country is the white man's worst fear – angry black men.

Help us to help you put the Great back into Britain. Together let's aim to build Britain into a better and safer country. Join with us to campaign, educate and stamp out the ugly scourge of

RACISM.

Vaz Littleford, the editor, was more than pleased with Marcia's copy. It said what there was to say, drawing on the reality of the lives of most black people of the time. It was written with feeling, directness and accuracy. Her editor gave her his comments and asked her whether she would be interested in learning to cover political issues for the paper. It would mean shadowing the political editor but he knew that soon she would be in a position to work on her own, covering party political conferences and all new policy changes.

Marcia accepted the compliments with pleasure and she knew that she deserved every word of his praise, but while she knew that politics affected her and everybody else's life, she told him firmly that wasn't the direction in which she wanted to go journalistically. He explained that it would be beneficial for her to begin to specialise in an area that she found interesting and stimulating.

But Marcia didn't even have to think twice about it. The world of glamour was what she wanted to cover. Although she herself was very good-looking and tall, she wasn't interested in being the person who people talked or wrote about. In her time as a journalist she'd already learned that they were not the ones with power. The real power was in the pen, and she wanted to be the person holding it.

Vaz was disappointed in Marcia's choice of direction. Everybody looked at the world of entertainment as the area to get into because of its glamorous image, but he believed that Marcia had so much more to give. He saw great promise in her writing skill and tried to dissuade her from taking such an unoriginal route. He knew that she craved success and he pointed out that she was far more likely to achieve it in politics than elsewhere because there was much less competition.

'I suppose you're right,' agreed Marcia, 'but I know I'm just not the kind of person who's going to go all out in that area and turn things around. I have aspirations in another direction. I always have had. I have to follow my heart. You must understand that, Vaz.'

Vaz tried another tack. He agreed to her working on entertainment but, instead of utilising her unique talents for finding and writing stories, he sent her to cover concerts and review films instead. When major celebrities were in town, he'd send Pauline Miller or Georgette Thomas, two very average reporters, to the press conferences. If Marcia acted on her own initiative and suggested covering certain stories from interesting angles different from the route they all knew other papers would take, he still didn't let her do it. He made her sit down with another journalist and talk through her ideas. Vaz thought that if she was passed over enough times it would have the desired affect, but it didn't. Marcia stuck to her guns. She knew that work as a journalist was hard to come by: her only other option at this stage was to try to find work on a local level and she'd already experienced life on a local rag. She'd have to stay put, bide her time and pray that, eventually, Vaz would see things her way. But she'd been waiting for three months now. How long was it going to take him to give her a break?

16

Kent,
May 1984

As the newly elected MP for Hazelhurst in Kent, Peter was always in demand to speak at functions up and down the country. Later, as a rapidly promoted junior health minister, there were increasing requests for him to appear on news programmes, and he was becoming a familiar face on shows which debated the issues vital to all political parties vying for a soap-box on national television. He was fast becoming a mini celebrity. The public loved him because he was 'tele-visual', in other words he looked good on screen. His party loved him because the public did, and he loved the attention that his new-found fame had brought him.

Clare was used to Peter staying in London to work through the week and coming home only at weekends when he was a doctor, but these days there were many weekends when he didn't make it home at all. But a new Clare was emerging now that the children were older, and she was looking to other activities to satisfy her needs.

It all started because Clare was known among her friends as a brilliant cook. On one occasion she was asked to bake her own choice of desserts to be be sold at a fund-raising gala, the profits of which were going to charity. What she produced was received so warmly that it gave Clare what she used to feel when helping Peter – a real sense of purpose and a feeling of achievement. As a result, she began to organise fund-raising events of her own on a regular basis for well-known organisations or charities which she helped to initiate. In doing so, she had found something that she was really good at and now being the wife of an MP didn't just mean attending lots of different social gatherings. Clare took her new work very seriously and organised more events than she attended as a guest. As the initiator and leading light of many a charity appeal, over the last year she'd already raised over £700,000 in Britain and abroad.

Jake and Thomas attended the same exclusive private school, while Sarah was taken to a private nursery two days a week. The right to buy the type of education you wanted was what the Conservative Party stood for and, being children of an MP, they were bound to reap the benefits of their father's beliefs. They too were used to their father not being around, but his absence didn't seem to have any adverse effects on them academically or emotionally. They relied on their mother for everything and she was always there at the drop of a hat. She was successfully fulfilling a role as a good mother, charity organiser and housekeeper.

She collected her children at three-thirty each afternoon. Before or after she was either cooking, cleaning, on the telephone, typing, at a beauty salon or, like that particular morning, gardening. A constant gush of bubbling water spluttered out from the marble cherub-shaped fountain and into the wide pond full of imported tropical fish. They swam around in their modest surroundings unaware that their movements gave off a stunning kaleidoscopic effect. The multi-colours of their scales, orange, black, pink, green and blue, complemented the magnificent scenery of her garden, which housed the most beautiful shrubs and flowers, making it a plant lover's paradise. From a panoramic view, it was a shining example of horticultural genius applied to a space just one hundred feet by seventy-five. Her gardener had come recommended by the people from whom they bought the house. Gardening was a new passion of hers. It enabled her to use her creative, artistic eye and, as well as being a mother and fund-raiser, gave her something that was all-important: another purpose in life. Clare needed that. Occasionally, very occasionally, a tiny seed of doubt would creep into her's mind. Is my life worthwhile? she would ask herself. This may have been good enough for my mother but is it enough for me? Why do I sometimes feel so depressed? Wouldn't it be better if I had a job and was out in the world like Peter? Then she would shrug it off and tell herself not to be so stupid. She was very lucky to have such a charmed life.

It was a surprisingly beautiful May day and she decided not to waste the warmth of the sun. That afternoon a group of women were coming to discuss their latest fund-raising activity, a charity fashion show, and Clare decided to serve them tea in the garden she was so proud of. They were all wives of doctors, solicitors, architects and MPs and, like Clare, they had very comfortable lifestyles. But it was important to them all to give something back to those less fortunate than themselves.

Clare passed around the lightly buttered scones to the ladies assembled on her patio and acknowledged the compliments.

Finally one woman said, 'Clare, you know, it really isn't fair at all. Here you are, you've got everything, a beautiful home, a garden to die for, well-mannered children, a wonderful, caring husband. I mean, what more could a woman possibly want?'

Clare could remember asking herself the very same question. Peter didn't realise the strain that playing the ideal couple was actually putting her under. She knew how important it was for an MP to exude security, and how better to do it than with a seemingly happy family, but her marriage, or at least being seen to be happily married, was equally important to her. Clare would have been devastated if her friends or the general public ever discovered how bad things were between her and Peter! Her pride would be deeply wounded. She couldn't stand the thought of people knowing that her husband, the man whom many of them fancied themselves and certainly respected, wasn't sleeping with her any more and in fact was barely communicating with her. There seemed to be nothing left between them nowadays but as long as they could keep up the pretence, as long as he turned up at her charity events and seemed fully to support her in all her endeavours, and as long as he needed her to attend party functions with him, it would all be fine.

Clare left her guests exclaiming over the vivid display of flowers in her garden, multi-coloured roses, deep purple clematis, bright red tulips and yellow primroses, and went to make more tea. Walking up the pathway to the house, she congratulated herself on yet another successful social afternoon. She had been able to keep up the facade of a happy and successful housewife and they had loved what she had prepared for them. As soon as she got back from making more tea they'd get down to the work of organising the next show that they had in mind. There was so much to do and now, so little time; but first things first. She'd have to make a call and see whether Googie was free to help put on this charity fashion parade, because when it came to PR she was the best. And Clare wanted everything to look the best in her outside world even if her inside one was crumbling.

17

Ealing,
1984

'Tiffany, can you go for a fitting this morning? They need models for a charity do tonight, darling. The money's not great, £300, and I know that you booked yourself out for a few days, but I want you to do it because there'll be a lot of influential people there. Can you go, darling?'

Tiffany was still in bed when her agent called. Drowsily, she mulled over what she was supposed to do that day. She couldn't think of anything that would stop her and she needed to remain in her head booker's good books.

'Yeah, I don't see why not. What's the time?'

'It's ten past nine, darling. Did you have a late night?'

'Yeah, sort of. What time do I need to be there?'

'Midday. You'll have a fitting, then they'll choreograph the routines. Show starts at six-thirty, you'll be out by eight.'

'Where is it? Where do I have to get to?'

'They're doing the casting in a marquee which is where the fashion show's going to take place. It's actually at the back of the organiser's home in Kent. Must be very plush, darling. I'm going to organise a car.'

'Why's it such a late call?'

'Oh, that's Googie. She always books models at the last moment so that she can get a better deal. She . . .' The office phone rang in the background. 'Tiff, I have to get that. There's no-one else in the office at the moment. Darling, the car will be there at eleven, OK? I'll speak to you later.'

'I'll be ready.'

As she draped her legs over the side of her bed, Tiffany immediately started to think about what she was going to wear. She heard the front door close. Grace was back from taking Chantelle to school. She popped her head around Tiffany's bedroom door.

'Oh, you're up already? I thought you'd be sleeping till at least noon.'

'I would love to have slept all day since I didn't get in from that party until about four this morning, but Stella just called about a job for tonight.'

'But I thought that you'd decided to take time off and spend it with Chantelle? Didn't you tell her yesterday that you were going to pick her up from school and take her out tonight?'

'That was the plan, but . . . I can't say no to Stella. You know how it goes. I'll make it up to her. Actually, it won't be a late night. I should be back before she goes to bed. I can take Chantelle out tomorrow She'll be OK.'

'Oh, I'm sure she'll be OK,' Grace affirmed, full of relief that Tiffany wasn't going to be able to get her hands on her daughter and possibly undo the damage that she was single-handedly cultivating. 'You go and live your life. You know that I'm here with Chantelle giving her the best care and attention. She'll be fine.'

Clare had spent the previous day and that morning catering for the evening's event. She'd packed everything in her car, got dressed in one of her smartest outfits and collected her children from school. They were coming with her to the show and Peter was going to be brought straight there from the House of Commons, to show support to his wife.

When Clare arrived, she let the hired staff unload her car and then headed for the marquee set up at the back of Googie's home to catch the end of the rehearsals with the choreographer, putting the models through their paces.

Clare wanted to greet the models and thank them for giving their time and effort to her appeal. She was well aware of the fee negotiated by Googie for each model and knew that they would usually have been paid much more for what effectively was going to take up a whole day. As she went to shake Tiffany's hand their eyes met and, instead of a smile forming, a cold chill ran through Clare's body. Without a stitch of make-up, the woman facing her was an absolute vision of beauty. Unlike the other models, who were stunning enough, this one took Clare's breath away. But before she could work out what it was in particular that struck her about Tiffany, the children came running up and were pulling at her dress and asking whether they too could model on the stage.

Tiffany left Clare hugging her children. It was ironic that these two women each saw something in the other that she envied. The image of a loving mother with her children, that surely was what success was all about, thought Tiffany. That was what being a mother should really mean. She knew where she should have been that evening, and she resolved to stop her relationship with Chantelle from deteriorating any further. When she got back that night, she would start to put things right immediately.

Peter had just arrived and he and his assistant Richard were led to their seats in the front row alongside other dignitaries and members of the press. He had no interest in the world of fashion. He was only there because his wife had absolutely insisted on it. As far as he was concerned, all models were bimbos. Over the past few years he'd met quite a few, since he was constantly being invited to celebrity galas. He was as good as a star himself: everyone knew who he was and his arrival always prompted a ripple of conversation between all the other guests.

The marquee seated 150 of this affluent town's most wealthy inhabitants. A lavish set incorporating flowers, sparkling fabrics and fluorescent lights illuminated the back of the stage and ran down both sides of the long cat-walk. Once everyone was seated, the compère announced the opening of the show. The black and white curtains drawn across the entrance of the catwalk swayed, rolled and then rose as music heralded a magnificent introduction. One by one, eight models appeared, dressed in black and white daywear, and began to perform a skilfully choreographed routine. The last model on the catwalk was Tiffany.

The designer labels included Armani, Saint-Laurent and Karl Lagerfeld, and as they were paraded it wasn't just Tiffany's colour that made her stand out from the rest. Although the only black model, she was also something special: she had class and charisma all of her own and knew how to use her slim, five foot ten frame. Her distinctive features were accentuated by her shiny black hair, which was swept back off her face and standing high in a bun on the crown of her head.

Everyone noticed her: it was hard not to. As she walked down the centre of the catwalk and turned her face towards the audience, even Peter Duvall MP, Mr Cool, Suave and Sophisticated, was gobsmacked.

The designs were spectacular, ranging from strong, dramatic black, white and red to delicate pastel shades of pink and mint green, culminating in the glitter and sparkle of gold and silver evening wear. As Googie walked down the catwalk followed by the models the audience applauded them all, but Peter's applause was only for Tiffany.

Drinks were being served and a buffet was laid out on

Googie's spacious patio which led into the marquee. As everyone mingled, laughter and chatter echoed through the crowd of fashion editors, actors, well-known charity organisers and famous faces from the world of entertainment.

'Wine?' asked Peter as he handed a glass to Tiffany who, unlike the other models, was already on her way home, bags in one hand, jacket and make-up case in the other. She had to get home to Chantelle to make a start at putting things right.

'I'm sorry, I've got to dash. I . . .' Her sentence remained unfinished as she looked up into his deep, dark brown eyes. She'd seen him sitting in the front row. He was striking to look at. She was definitely interested in talking to this man but her interests didn't extend to politics or even news and current affairs. She wondered who he was. He seemed to have a glint in his eye which was as good as an invitation to dinner. She needed to get home, but first there was no harm in just a quick chat.

'Wine?' Peter repeated. He was well aware of the effect that he had on most women.

'Yes . . . please,' Tiffany said, her eyes never leaving his. She grabbed at the glass forgetting that she had her make-up case in her hand. It landed on Peter's foot and the contents spilled on to the floor.

'Well, that broke the ice,' he said as he hopped about on one foot in agony. They both began to laugh and as they crouched down to retrieve Tiffany's belongings, they had a very brief conversation about the origin of her name, how old she was and which agency she was with. As they were about to stand up their eyes locked again and, between them, they knew. They both felt that certain something, a chemistry which immediately drew them together.

But Peter was a married man with three children. He was a member of parliament. Already he was thinking about his public image. Already he was looking over his shoulder to check who was watching.

He slipped her one of his cards and told her to call. Maybe he could have just one more dalliance in his life? Just one night was all he wanted. He'd never been unfaithful with a black chick before, never even considered it. But while he had been watching Tiffany on the catwalk that was all he was able to think about, although he had to admit he had been thinking with his body rather than his mind. Tiffany Ideh was a model, black and what he thought of as a bimbo, all the things that were taboo to a man like him, but right now he wasn't going to think about that. He had to have her.

Peter couldn't believe that he was actually doing this, spending so much time thinking about a black model he had only met once. He had waited all day for her call but now it was six-thirty and he knew it just wasn't going to happen. He could vividly remember the way she walked, looked, smiled, talked, even how she smelled. Why hadn't she called him? He'd had numerous affairs since Sally Crimson. She was now married and living in the States. Their relationship had lasted three months and had actually been very helpful to him in more ways than one. It had taught him how to have an affair and the rules that went with infidelity. He learned how and when to lie, and how to cover his traces. Since he no longer even had an affectionate relationship with Clare it was very easy to get away with it. She never got close enough to smell another woman's perfume.

His second affair was with his first secretary when he got to the House, Miss Sylvia Little. She'd been so happy to be given a job by him and had seduced him almost, he felt, to say thank you. He hadn't put up much resistance and, as with Sally, they had spent time working and travelling around the country together. Their eight-month affair had run its natural course. Clare was still none the wiser, his children hadn't been affected, so affairs, Peter believed, were the ideal solution to their marital problems. He needed a wife for his image, but she didn't seem to need sex the way he did. This way, no-one was getting hurt but he knew he'd have to be fairly careful about whom he selected. All he had to do was tell each woman he wanted to sleep with that he loved his wife and children, then it would be up to them whether they got involved with him or not. Sylvia had wanted to but now it was over and she had moved on to be a personal assistant to a front bench minister. They often saw each other in the vast expanse of corridor at the House, and they still had a mutual respect for each other, but their affair would always remain a secret between them.

Gwen Furrow was his third bit on the side. She was one of his researchers, but they were from the same background. They knew what to expect from the relationship and in the end there'd been no scandal and no pain on either side, but the fourth one, Hazel May, had wanted everything. The stupid woman really thought that one day he was going to give up everything and move in with her! She had great tits, but that was it. He'd had to get rid of her fast. She had fallen in love with him. The situation had developed into a potential time bomb and it would have been professional and personal suicide if he had waited for the explosion.

Then, of course, there had been the one-night stands. But this woman, Tiffany Ideh, what exactly would he be getting into with her? Why was he even bothering to think of one night of rampant sex with her when she hadn't even bothered to pick up the telephone to call?

He'd always believed in nothing ventured, nothing gained, so it was definitely worth making an effort. He'd get his secretary to find the number of her agency and call. No! That would involve too many people. He couldn't have anyone knowing. He'd just have to find the number himself. It shouldn't be too difficult. Tiffany Ideh was an unusual name. He could only hope that fate had dealt him a fair hand and that she wasn't ex-directory.

'Hello.'

'Can I speak to Tiffany Ideh, please?'

'Who's speaking?'

There was a brief pause and then he said, 'Peter. Peter Duvall.'

'What? Like, Peter Duvall, MP?'

'Look, is Tiffany there?'

'Yeah, of course she is. Hold on a minute, I'll just get her to pick up the other phone.'

As Tiffany picked up the receiver, Grace deeply regretted saying that she was in. Listening in on their coversation, she heard them chatting almost intimately and arranging to meet for dinner the following evening. Tiffany was excited when she replaced the handset and joined Grace in the sitting room. A wide smile was emblazoned across her face and she gave her sister a big hug in celebration of her feelings. 'For so long I've been down, Grace, but now everything is changing. He's lovely, Grace, you should see him. He's tall, intelligent and good-looking to boot.'

'Has he got any children?'

'Yep. Three.'

'So he's married, then?'

'I don't know. He didn't talk about a wife. Oh, what does it matter? Wives just didn't come up but I suppose we can talk about that tomorrow. Grace? Oh Lord, I don't even know what I'm going to wear. You might wonder why I'm going on like this, but you really should have seen him and we just . . . I can't explain it. D'you know what, though, I think that this might be the start of something big, Sis, it really might.'

'Did you tell him about Chantelle?' Grace yelled after her as she ran into the bedroom to rifle through her wardrobe.

'Give us a chance. We're only going out to dinner, we're not getting married.'

'Oh, I know that,' Grace whispered. 'I could have told you that.'

Peter called Tiffany in the morning.

'I needed to hear your voice even though I'll be seeing you tonight, and I needed to explain something. I hope you'll understand.'

'Yes?' Tiffany tried to keep the panic out of her voice. What did he have to tell her?

'Because of my . . . because I'm a member of parliament and I have a certain reputation to uphold, you know we have to be discreet. If people see us having dinner they'll put two and two together and come up with twenty-two. So can we meet in a hotel suite? Do you know the Searles Hotel? In Mayfair?'

He arrived fifteen minutes before her. The suite, as he had ordered, looked very romantic. Through the doorway he could just see the edge of the king-size bed which he hoped they'd wind up putting to good use before the night was out. That way the cost of the suite until noon the next day would be justified.

Tiffany gently rapped on the door. He opened it and then stood back to let her enter. She was wearing a red all-in-one body-hugging catsuit which flared at the bottom and was held together by a long central zip. Peter's eyes were drawn to her breasts which were large and rounded. She walked to the table, admiring the flowers and ornaments, the four large silver platters covering their meal.

Peter closed the door, walked towards her and stood there for a while, just looking. She stared back at him. It was obvious what was going to happen between them.

Gently, he pulled her towards him. She said nothing. All day she had been trying to come to terms with what she was letting herself in for. Having been told that a hotel suite was booked for their dinner as opposed to maybe a table in a small restaurant on the outskirts of London, she couldn't say that she didn't know how the evening was likely to turn out. Since Perry's imprisonment she'd been on a few dates with men from different races, but she hadn't had sex with any of them. She hadn't wanted to. But when she first saw Peter she had known what would happen with him.

Putting his hand around her head, he tilted it towards his and began to kiss her, first on the lips and neck and then lower, down the front of her catsuit. Tiffany didn't resist. Peter began gently to rub her nipples through her clothing, making her moan softly with pleasure, and soon she found herself responding, kissing him back, running her fingers through his thick, black hair and rubbing her hand on his trousers, against his growing penis. Soon Tiffany's breasts were exposed and Peter immediately began to kiss, lick and suck them as he led her over to the bed, trying to tear off the rest of her clothes on the way. But Tiffany wanted to savour the moment. She hadn't had sex for a long time and she didn't see that there was any need to rush. She wanted their evening to be special. She was aware that what she was about to embark on could just turn out to be a fling, a one-night stand, so she wanted it to last more than just five minutes. Love-making, Perry had taught her, was all about giving your partner pleasure; that was even more important than pleasing yourself, so first she'd tantalise him a little more, slowly undressing, but leaving on just her knickers. She began to undress him, undoing his buttons, sliding his shirt and jacket off, continually teasing and kissing him. What she was doing was working, he was becoming very aroused, but for Peter it was all happening much too slowly. He wanted her and he wanted her now.

Tiffany pushed him back against the wall, undid his belt and zip and pulled his trousers down, amazed by the huge bulge in his pants. Weren't white men's dicks supposed to be two inches long?

She held his penis and manipulated it almost like a pump, so much so that he was in danger of coming without even entering her and he didn't want that.

He pulled her back on to the bed. She rolled over and sat on top of him as he lay flat and guided his penis inside her. She had a beautiful body, her waist curved in, her breasts were pert and firm. She gyrated her hips in slow rhythmic circles, stretching her arms behind her to lightly squeeze his balls. It felt so good but he had to stop her making him come too soon. Right now, with his eyes wide open, watching this vision of black beauty, he was experiencing a feeling that he'd never had before and he wanted it to last for as long as possible.

He held on to her hand and, guiding her to lie down, he kissed her mouth and her face, mounting and entering her. Usually on a first date, his aim was to just reach a climax as soon as possible. It was only when his feelings for the woman had grown that he began to care about her enjoyment. But this woman was different. She was making him contemplate doing things he had never done before.

He didn't want that night ever to end. She'd resisted putting his dick in her mouth, but he wanted to taste her. He slid out of her and wriggled down her body to open up her legs. She smelt of love, it was a sweet aroma and he wanted to taste it too. She moved around with the thrill of his tongue brushing gently against the path of her vagina. His warm breath followed the trail that he was making, up and down and around. He kissed her all over as he turned her on to her belly. His kisses followed the divide that separated her buttocks and he continued up her back, moving her hair out of the way and caressing and lightly biting her neck. Once fully on top of her again, he entered her. Placing his hands under each of her breasts, he squeezed them. Their movements increased until, eventually, they came together.

He had planned to make it a one-night stand but he knew he had to stay in contact with any woman who made him feel as good as this.

And he did.

18

Kent, March 1985

Clare sat in the dark in the study on yet another long and lonely night. She pulled her woollen shawl tightly around her shoulders and tied the ends to keep the fit snug. She certainly hadn't got married to do this every night: put the children to bed and then keep her own company. It had been such a long time since there had been any intimacy between Peter and herself. Once they had been dubbed the beautiful couple, yet it had been well over two years since they last made love. Where had it all gone wrong?

There was hardly any communication. He didn't share his problems with her about his work. They never went out and the last time he'd attended one of Clare's charity events was the fashion show nearly a year ago. He was always so busy, the children hardly ever saw him and her failure as a wife, as she saw it, was getting her down. It had reached the stage where she was the one suggesting they make love, throwing herself at him even though she didn't feel like it, and what made it even worse was that he was rejecting her. He didn't want her any more – on any level.

She felt he believed that as long as he paid the bills he

was being a good husband and father, but now that the children were growing up she needed more from him than that. She used to get a buzz out of being needed, both at home and in her fund-raising. Now it meant nothing without the approbation of one man. Without her husband's acknowledgement and encouragement, was any of it worthwhile? How could she cheerfully try to help put other people's houses in order when her own was falling apart? She still loved Peter but it was plain to see that his love for her was fading. Quite clearly she was now a wife in name only, for the benefit of his career.

She'd been worried about the state of her marriage for some time and spoke to her mother about it, as it was from her that Clare had learned what a successful marriage was supposed to entail. Her mother's solution to the whole problem was very simple. She advised Clare to lose some weight. She felt that maybe Peter would like to have back the woman he married, not someone who was more than double her size. She believed that this was the root of all their problems. How could Peter possibly find Clare attractive in her current state?

'Sex is very important in marriage,' Clare's mother advised her daughter. 'If need be, go to your doctor for some pills to curb your appetite. It's all that cooking you used to do for your charity events that's to blame, I suppose, but you could do something about it quickly, get started now, and in a couple of months everything will be back to normal.'

'Oh, Mother! That's not . . . Look, I admit that there is a lack of activity in our bedroom, but that's got nothing to do with my weight gain!' Clare sighed. 'Peter's hardly ever here any more and on the very few occasions when he is I just haven't been in the mood.'

Mary gave her a look which said that she'd guessed as much. Although she felt sorry for her daughter, just sympathising wasn't going to help. 'Maybe you could ask the doctor for something to help get you in the mood more often? I shouldn't have to tell you this, dear, but whatever you do, you must satisfy your husband in the bedroom.'

Her mother's comments only added to Clare's lack of self-respect. But she still had some strength, she wasn't powerless to try to put her marriage back on the right track. And she knew she had to act fast.

Her first move was to speak to Peter. She'd looked in the diary that he kept at home and seen that the next three weeks were packed with several trips out of the country. She would wait until he next telephoned and tackle him then.

But when the phone rang on that Friday evening at the same time Peter always called, Clare felt scared. She knew exactly what she had to say, the questions to ask, the mood to be in. After the sixth ring, she picked up the receiver and answered his mundane questions about the children and how they were getting along, but she was desperate to get beyond this superficial banter. She had to take control and shift the tone of it all. She began by asking him how he felt about their marriage. Was he aware that there had been such a deterioration in their relationship, which presently consisted of just a couple of telephone conversations a week? He was always asking after the children but how much did he really care if he was never around to see them? If their marriage was ever going to be worth anything more than just what was printed on their certificate, they both needed to put more work into it.

She kept Peter on the phone for what seemed like ages, pouring her heart out to him and taking most of the blame for the failure. She ended by suggesting that she accompany him on one of his many overseas trips so that, after he had dealt with business, they could stay on for a few more days and make it a second honeymoon.

Peter was making the call from his hotel room in St Moritz and Tiffany finally came out of the bathroom where she'd been applying her make-up. They were about to go out to dinner and she looked beautiful in a sequinned Frank Usher cocktail dress, her hair up in a French pleat. He had been listening to Clare and she wasn't telling him anything he didn't already know. She was quite right to take the blame for what had happened between them. If, after having Sarah, Clare's appetite for sex hadn't diminished in the way that it had, maybe he wouldn't have had that first affair with Sally Crimson and maybe things would have been different? He was only a man after all, and all men had desires that had to be taken care of. And right now there was no-one better than Tiffany to do that for him.

He pointed to the phone and put his finger to his lips to silence Tiffany. Peter watched her as she moved about the room and he knew that this was the woman he wanted to be with.

Peter dismissed Clare's offer of a second honeymoon with the excuse that his mind wouldn't be on his work if she came. But her talk with him did achieve something, although it couldn't have been further from what she wanted. It made Peter realise that his marriage had to end, and the sooner the better. He knew in his heart what he had to do and no matter how guilty hearing Clare pour out her heart had made him feel, he had to admit it was over. He would point out to her that she had admitted it in her phone call. Why should they try to reinvent something that was dead and had been for years? He would have to make her see that he should be allowed to find true love and happiness with someone else.

It was time to bring Tiffany out into the spotlight and present her as the woman of his dreams to the rest of the world! He knew that if he did that he would have so much to face and so much to lose, but how much longer would Tiffany put up with being in a clandestine relationship with him? She wanted more and she deserved more. If he let the world know about his ten-month affair, his actions would show Tiffany just how serious he was. If he didn't see her even for a few hours, his heart ached. He wanted her by his side every single day for the rest of his life, but the thought of the repercussions such a step could have on his life and his career was giving him an awful migraine.

For example, what would Clare's father say? He'd have to face the music from the man he respected as much as his own father. If Graham were ever to catch wind of his liaison with Tiffany, Peter would be dead meat: he'd be ruined politically and professionally, that was for sure. Of course he'd made a lot of contacts of his own as a doctor and MP, but Graham had far more influence than he did, even now. Peter could never forget that he owed much of his success in life to his father-in-law.

Then there were his constituents. They would certainly have a say regarding his future. How would they take it? Many an MP had had an extra-marital affair, but how many had survived?

But his love for Tiffany was growing stronger and stronger every day. The time to remain silent had passed. He was no longer going to keep his true feelings and his mistress locked away like something dirty and shameful. After all, it really just boiled down to a man falling out of love with his wife and falling in love with someone else.

A week later, as he sat through an important conference in Brussels, his concentration was elsewhere. Graham wasn't necessarily going to be the biggest problem he'd have to face. He also pondered on the response of the tabloids when his secret life with Tiffany became public knowledge. He knew that the press would initially jump on the fact that she was black and would talk about her profession in a sordid manner, but he'd convinced her to give up the modelling months earlier and was now giving her financial support.

It was just as well that the Harley Street practice set up

by Clare's father was such a gold mine or Peter would be in serious financial trouble. As it was, he didn't know how much longer he could meet the expenses of his double life. All Tiffany had to do was ask and it was hers, like the Mercedes sports she now drove. No doubt the tabloids would also find out about that! The British press were really ruthless when they wanted to be and deserved the worldwide tag of being the sleaziest. He would be hounded relentlessly and as for his children, his poor children! He could imagine the gutter press camping outside their school gates and harrassing them. What could explode as a result of his love for another woman was a living nightmare. Reflecting on the likely reaction of the press, all he could do was promise himself that the next time a privacy bill was tabled, he would use his vote wisely regardless of the pressure from the Whips.

The conference was looking into the health care systems used by different European countries. The citizens of his own were becoming afraid that Britain would soon adopt the American ideology, where a person's life is only as important as the size of their bank account or insurance cover. The British were mindful and resentful of this seemingly gradual move of the Government towards some type of health insurance scheme. To the people it was a frightening prospect, and Peter's brief was to gather the even more frightening realities and statistics of other countries' health care policies, so that they could be used as standard defence jargon for the Conservatives when the subject and arguments were raised. He had listened to very little and written down even less. His mind was elsewhere. He had to take the plunge and speak to Clare because now he had something to ask Tiffany, and something to give her.

Tiffany had been working non-stop before her association with Peter, but now her life was busy in other ways. It was full of shopping sprees, beauty parlours, foreign trips and eating out at discreet restaurants with Peter for breakfast, lunch and dinner. She had had success as a model on a small scale before, but now she had access to large amounts of money. She had changed. She couldn't help it. Her life was centred around Peter. There were no family members or friends to keep her grounded, no-one except Grace who only encouraged her to keep up the life she was living even if that meant leaving Chantelle behind. As for Chantelle, Tiffany believed that she knew what she was doing. From her first date with Peter, her instinct had told her to keep quiet about the fact that she had a child, otherwise she would lose him. He was special. There would come a time when she could tell him about Chantelle but it was important that she wait for the right moment.

But she kept putting it off. First she told herself that she didn't know how long the affair was going to last and it wouldn't be fair to involve Chantelle too soon. Then she began to panic that she would lose Peter if she told him and by the time she realised that he was serious about her, she also recognized the fact that the last thing he needed to be saddled with was the cliché of a black single mother.

Now it was too late. She couldn't just come out with, 'Oh, by the way, I've got a child . . .'

In anticipation of the day when she would pluck up the courage, Tiffany composed a song, which she was going to record just for him and play when they were alone. But although she wrote the words, she never got around to giving it to him. Besides, Grace said that it was a stupid idea.

> Before you fall in love with me
> There's something I must say ·
> It makes no difference when I do
> The matter won't go away
> I'm talking about my child

There's something that you must do
Before you fall in love with me
You must want my child too.

Love me, love my child
The fact is that I am a mother
Love me, love my child
One doesn't come without the other
Maybe there's no need to say it,
But I think that you should know
That if you love me, love my child
Our relationship can only grow.

He'd never been to her flat and had never really wanted to. It suited him fine not to have to get out of his car and for Tiffany to meet him downstairs when he picked her up, although more often than not he'd send a car for her or she would drive herself. He did often wonder, at the beginning of their relationship, why she had never invited him up. 'You haven't got a husband or boyfriend tucked away up there, have you?' he would ask jokingly. After all, she was a beautiful young woman who, when they met, was apparently free and single: he couldn't believe his luck. It was some time before he was totally convinced that there was no-one else in her life.

On the night of the Brussels conference they had dinner at a restaurant not far from their five-star hotel. When Peter presented a spectacular, dazzling diamond engagement ring to Tiffany she was stunned. How could he be giving her an engagement ring when he was already married to someone else?

What would her life have been like if she hadn't allowed him to make love to her on their first date? He was so good-looking, how could she have refused? What more could a woman want? Actually she knew the answer to that. A woman in her right mind would want a man who wasn't married. A man who could realistically meet the commitments behind his proposal. From what Peter had told her about his wife in the past, she knew that Clare's marriage vows meant a lot to her. How easily would she accept the fact that the marriage was over?

'Peter, I don't understand. How can you . . . ?'

'Understand this, darling. I love you, I love you more than I've ever loved anyone and I don't care any more about the consequences. You're the one I want to be with, and when we get back to London . . . I'm going to talk to Clare. I'm going to tell her all about us and then . . . then I'm going to leave her. I'm leaving her and my children, even though I love them dearly. I'm doing all of this because of the love that I have for you. Now can you imagine how much you mean to me? I know that it will take some time for the divorce to come through, but when it does, I want to marry you. Tiffany? Just tell me that you love me and that you want me, then I know I'll be able to find the strength that I'm going to need to face everybody.'

His words were very impressive. Was he really about to give up everything for her?

'Peter, I do love you, but I also know what you're going to have to go through, so I . . .'

'Don't say another word, Tiffany. I know exactly what you're going to say, but don't doubt me. I've told you how I feel and I'm serious. Hey,' he placed his fingers under her chin and raised it. 'I promise you that I will make everything all right. Just love me the way that you've been doing and trust me.'

She did love him and she did trust him. Her mind was racing but she really didn't have anything to be fearful of. As far as she was concerned, from this moment on Peter Duvall was going to be her future. There was no need to resist for another second; there was no need to spoil this moment with any more negative thoughts. Right now, she considered herself to be the luckiest woman in the world. She would accept his proposal. The fact that he already had a wife was his problem and his problem alone. She'd just have to be there for him when he needed her.

Back in their hotel room Tiffany rushed to the phone. 'Do you have to phone now? I thought that we could just go to bed to celebrate our future. It's very late, you know.'

'I have to speak to my sister. You go ahead and run a bath for us. I won't be long.'

Grace came on the line as Peter disappeared into the bathroom and Tiffany could hear the sound of water running into the tub.

'Hi, Grace, how are things?'

'Fine, fine. And you? How are things there?'

'Wonderful. We're coming back to London for two days but, can you believe it, we're going to the Bahamas next week. It's just been great, Sis, and wait for it . . . Pete bought me a diamond engagement ring!'

Grace was stunned into silence.

'I know what you're thinking – that he's not divorced yet, but he's going to put a divorce in motion as soon as we get back.'

'But haven't you ever thought that you're taking away another woman's man? He's not your husband!'

'I'm surprised that you're saying that. You know full well that their relationship had broken down long before I came on the scene.'

'Yeah, you and your long legs.'

'What did you say? I've got the bath running here and it isn't a brilliant line.'

'Oh, nothing!'

'Right, well, the ring's just to show me that as soon as his divorce comes through we're going to get married. Oh, let me speak to Chantelle and tell her the good news.'

'Chantelle's sleeping. It's after midnight, you know? And what exactly do you think you're doing, waking her up to tell her you're going to marry a man who doesn't even know she exists?'

'Oh . . . but isn't it a special occasion? Well, we'll be back on Sunday anyway. I'll be home by eight in the evening the latest, and on Monday,' Tiffany looked over her shoulder to make sure that Peter wasn't around to hear her next words, 'I'm going to introduce Peter to Chantelle.'

'So you've finally told him.'

'Well, not exactly.'

'You mean you still haven't . . . well, hey, the truth is, if he really loves you it won't make any difference.'

'I hope that you're right, Grace.'

'I usually am.'

Grace didn't mention her hope that the news about Tiffany's daughter would ruin her sister's relationship.

'. . . but you must tell him. Tell him tonight.'

'I will. I will.'

But Tiffany didn't want to spoil the romantic time they were having. She knew that he loved her, so everything would be all right. On Monday evening, after he had spoken to his wife and people at the House, they were going to dinner at Langan's and she decided she would take Chantelle along and say, 'Hey, Pete, meet my daughter, our daughter.' He had three children who she was more than willing to accept because she loved him. Surely he would feel the same about her child? How could he not? Chantelle was so beautiful. Everything would be OK. She had a good feeling about it.

As Grace put the phone down Chantelle, who had woken up, tugged at Grace's dressing gown and asked sleepily, 'Who was that? Why was the phone ringing so late, Aunty Grace? Was that Mummy?'

'Yes, Chan. But I'm afraid that she didn't have time to speak to you.'

19

Lowestoft Prison, 1985

In the cold light of day, they just looked like cream-coloured bricks in the eight- by six-foot cell. The colours were designed to help inmates meditate and calmly reflect, but it was strange how a few pulls on a spliff made the paint-covered cracks look more like snakes trying to squeeze their way out of the wall and break free. Perry might no longer be selling drugs to inmates but they were certainly always readily available and he had enough cash stashed away to purchase whatever he wanted.

The establishment had got it so wrong. Did they really think that locking people up for years and years was a deterrent against committing further crimes? A month into his sentence, Perry would have done anything to get away from the volatile atmosphere in Brixton and the stifling lack of liberty. At that stage he would never have reoffended again, but as time went on he got used to it. He began to adjust and before long he was mixing with other criminals who passed on the benefit of their experience. Instead of an environment for reform, prison was simply the best training ground for criminal activity.

Time dragged at Lowestoft, especially after Perry received Tiffany's letter telling him she couldn't handle the situation any longer and wanted out. She said she no longer loved him and that hurt, but he felt sure he could convince her otherwise. It was so frustrating. If only he could see her and talk to her, but what hope did he have of that until his release date if she wouldn't come to see him? It had been over a year since he had heard from her and despite all the times he had written and sent visiting orders, she hadn't responded once.

Now Perry had a letter. He stretched out on his single padded mattress. He wanted to get comfortable to enjoy this treat. He didn't usually receive mail. In fact he'd hoped, when he'd heard about it, that it was from Tiffany, but it wasn't her hand-writing on the envelope. Ready and relaxed, he began to read slowly and deliberately, trying to savour every word.

'Perry – Walker. B–2–5–7–2–2. G – Wing – Blunderston – Lowestoft – Suffolk. Yep, it's for me.'

Perry read the letter once and then he read it again. Someone was coming to see him, the last person he had expected to see, someone who said they had important news for him.

He was going to have a visitor.

20

Kent,
Early April 1985

Peter planned to speak to Clare and tell her everything – she had to be the first to know – before he faced the Chief Whip at the House. As Peter was a very popular MP there was bound to be a great deal of press interest when everything came to light. It was the Whip's job to try to lessen the blow to the Government and he knew that the PM would definitely be informed, as would the leader of his constituency party. And then of course he had to speak personally to his private secretary. Peter had a busy and difficult day ahead of him and later that Monday evening he was due to meet Tiffany at Langan's, where they hoped to start celebrating the first day of their public relationship.

Tiffany was also planning her own surprise celebration with the introduction of Chantelle.

Peter didn't want the children around when he spoke to Clare, and he told her so. She was excited to hear that he wanted to have a talk with her. It had been such a long time since he'd actually instigated a discussion between them and it could only be good news. It was over a week since she had spoken to him about how she felt about their marriage, long enough for him to have had time to reflect. As she drove the children to school, she felt glad that she had raised her worries and fears. Even with all that had happened between them, she still loved her husband. This morning could be the start of something new and fresh. He wanted to sort their problems out. The fact that he didn't want the children to be around surely meant that he wanted them to make love.

On her return, she heard Peter in the kitchen. She'd leave him undisturbed while she slipped upstairs to change for him. She still had that long black silk negligee he'd bought her for Christmas maybe as many as six years ago. She'd never worn it, but this was the perfect occasion to christen it.

He was slouched in an armchair with a glass of whisky when she made her entrance.

'It's a bit early for alcohol, isn't it, darling?' Clare tried to sound sexy and strike a provocative pose but one look at his face told her she wasn't making the right impression.

What he had to say didn't warrant either of them getting dressed for bed. He needed to talk to her, he needed to say what he had to say before she made a fool of herself and embarrassed them both.

'Clare . . .' he began, slowly yet very deliberately, but she ran over, kneeled in front of him, cupped his face in her hands and started to kiss him all over.

'I understand everything because I've been feeling it, too,' she said breathlessly. 'And I'm so glad you decided that we needed to talk about our marriage, about everything, before it totally got out of hand. I love you and I know that you love me: that's all that's important, Peter . . .' She slipped off her negligee and let it fall to the floor, then bent to undo the belt and zip on his trousers.

'Clare . . .' Peter managed between her slobbering kisses. 'Clare, I . . .'

'Sssh. There's no need for words right now. I want you. I want us to do this. Why did we allow things to get so bad before doing anything about it? Oh, Peter!

Peter tried to move his face away.

'Just relax, darling. I know that it's been a long time but we . . .'

'Clare! Stop!' Peter yelled, pushing her back. Clare sat back in shock.

'God! I tried to get you to stop, but you wouldn't listen, you just wouldn't listen.' Peter stormed over to the bay window. He didn't want to look at Clare; he knew she'd just be sitting there on the Axminster carpet, looking hurt and insecure. She was so different from Tiffany, the woman he loved. He knew that if Tiffany had been placed in the same predicament that Clare was in now, she wouldn't have simply sat there. She would have leapt up and poured the rest of the Scotch over him. And as for Clare trying to seduce him! Nowadays he believed that Clare couldn't turn on a gas cooker, much less stir up sexual passions in a real man like himself. He didn't want to look at her. He knew he would be disappointed with what he saw and he didn't want his last image of his wife to be a pathetic one. Instead he stared out at the magnificent floral splendour she had created in the garden.

'Well,' said Clare softly behind him, 'I'm listening.'

He'd had it all worked out, how he was going to start, what he was going to say. It wasn't entirely her fault, although she had blamed herself on the phone last week. It was a failure on both their parts, but mainly his. If he took most of the blame, maybe she would be easier to talk to. But as soon as he began, his prepared speech went out of the window.

'It all started because . . . well . . . the fact that you were never in the mood for making love. I used it as an excuse to . . . to have an affair.'

There. He had said it. Clare looked up sharply. She

hadn't known what to expect but it certainly wasn't this. Before she could respond he said the most devasting words she could possibly hear.

'Clare, I want a divorce.'

He carried on looking out of the window. Clare waited for him to turn round and face her. There stood the man of her dreams, her university sweetheart, her husband, but to him she had become obsolete. He didn't want her or need her any more. Why hadn't she guessed? How blind and stupid could she have been? If she wasn't making love to him over the past few years, he must have been getting it from somewhere. Maybe at the back of her mind she had known.

She thought about the implications, the people she'd have to explain things to, the questions they'd ask. Everyone would begin to see her as a failure and she couldn't face that right now. And what about their children? What was she supposed to say to them? What was she going to tell her parents? Her father had paved the way for Peter and this was his reward? There was too much to take in, there were too many hurtful issues to think about. One thing was certain: she wasn't going to give him a divorce. She'd fight that every step of the way, not just for her sake but for his. If he was having an affair, it couldn't have developed into anything serious, surely? It could only be an infatuation.

'Peter, look at me. Who is this woman? Where is she from? How did you meet her?' Clare's voice was taut with emotion.

'I don't think you really want to hear the answer to that.'

'I want to know everything.'

'OK, you asked for this. Can you remember, last May, when I came to that fashion show you organised at Googie's? Remember?'

'This has been going on since then?! Who the fuck is she, Peter?'

He had never heard Clare swear. He didn't understand why, but he suddenly felt nervous. He had no reason to fear Clare. He had every right to want out.

'Her name's Tiffany. Tiffany Ideh.'

'Tiffany Id . . . ? What type of a surname is that? What's her family background?'

Peter didn't answer straight away. He was well aware that this was going to be a bone of contention for many people.

'Well, her parents . . . she used to be . . . no, her parents first . . . they're from Nigeria. She's Nigerian, and Tiffany? She used to be a model. A fashion model.'

'She's what!? I can't believe this, Peter. Tell me it's not true and I'm the butt of a very bad joke!'

Peter was beginning to lose patience. He thought of all of the other people he had to talk to that day. He had a lot to do. Maybe Clare deserved more than this, but it was all perfectly clear. Nothing was going to change and he wanted to get a move on. The sooner she took in what he was telling her, the better.

'I'm leaving, Clare,' he said firmly. 'Our marriage is over and I want a divorce. I've fallen in love with someone else but that's not the reason why I have to go. The fact is, I've fallen out of love with you and if you face up to it you'll see I'm right.'

'You bastard. You selfish, overbearing, self-important bastard!'

'Clare. There's no need to . . .'

'There's no need for what, for fuck's sake? Are you crazy? Have you really lost you mind? I mean have you for a second really considered the consequences of what you're saying?'

'Of course I have. Look, I'm not some sort of love-sick puppy, you know. I've spent the best part of a year thinking about it.'

'You've been having your sordid little affair for that long?

Sleeping with your whore and still coming into this house and touching the children? My children! A year is nothing! What about our marriage? You've been a part of my life for fifteen years! Fifteen years, Peter!'

'Look, it doesn't mean that I don't love our children. I do. I just can't live . . .'

'How can you love our children? How can you do this to them? They don't deserve any of this. Don't you understand what you're doing, Peter?'

'If I could just have continued to live a lie, I suppose everything would have been all right, but I can't. It's not fair on anyone, you, the children, or Tiffa . . .'

'Don't you dare mention that woman's name in this house again! How could you?' she screeched. 'Look, I can forget all that you've just said to me today. I mean it, Peter. As far as I'm concerned, you haven't said anything about being in love with someone else, about a divorce, about wanting to leave us. You have to rethink everything. You say you love the children. Think about them and what it will do to them, think about your career. You'd have to resign, do you realise? You've worked so hard to get this far, we did it together, remember? I helped you, my father helped you. We were good together, Peter; a great team. Don't throw it all away. Don't.'

Clare had stepped forward and put her arms around her husband. He didn't pull back and she took this as a positive sign. 'We need a break,' she went on quickly. 'I suggested that before but you didn't want to then. Let's go away, Pete. Mother will have the children. We can sort our marriage out. You're just confused right now, and I know I haven't been the wife that I should have been recently; the wife that you deserve. Peter? I love you. Don't throw our marriage away. We deserve another chance. Peter? Give us that at least. Or maybe I should say, give *me* another chance.'

For a second Peter hesitated. He could see what he had

once been attracted to in her – a woman who was keen to please and would do everything she could to be successful as a wife. But what could he tell her now but the truth? Did she really want to continue to live with a man who no longer found her attractive or interesting? It was over. It didn't matter how he looked at it. From every conceivable angle, they were through.

She might be the same woman he had married but time hadn't stood still for him. His work, his association with other people, his travelling, his affairs had made it impossible for him to do anything but move on. Now he wanted much more from life than what he had with Clare. There was nothing new to talk about, nothing left for him to stay for; and the sooner he went the more comfortable he would feel.

'I'm sorry, Clare. I'm sorry for everything. Of course I'll look after you financially. You can stay in the house, I'll take care of all that. I don't know what else there is for me to say right now.' Peter gently moved Clare to one side as he walked towards the cupboard in the hallway. 'I've already packed. I have to move out now and I'll call you later about my other things. You need time to think. Tell me what you want. Whatever you want, I won't challenge it, it's yours.'

Clare followed him.

'Is that it? Is that all that I'm worth? Is that all that our marriage means to you? You've told me nothing. I want to know everything, Peter. You owe me that. Don't you think that you owe me at least that?'

'I'm not going to do this, Clare. I'm not going to stay here talking to you about intricate aspects of my relationship. You have to believe me when I say that my aim wasn't to hurt you with what I've just said, but to inform you of the facts.'

'What do you mean, you didn't want to hurt me? What do you think that you've just done? Made my fucking day?'

He turned away from her, opening the cupboard and

taking out three suitcases. He'd said enough. It was time to go.

'If you walk out of this door, Peter, I won't ever let you come back. Ever. How could you even think about leaving me for another woman, especially a black woman. She is black, isn't she, Peter, your Miss Idaya from Nigeria or whatever her bloody name is? Is what they say about black women really true then? That's what the attraction is, is it? You couldn't resist her black shiny skin, right? It wasn't enough for you to be an MP, to be a boss in professional terms, you wanted to find out how it felt to be the master, or should I say "massa"? Is that how she talks? Has she got a bit of a Jamaican accent? Eh?'

'I said that she was Nigerian, not Jamaican!'

'What's the difference? They all look alike, don't they?'

'Now you're just being ridiculous.'

'And what do you use in sex, Peter? Does she chain you up? Does she whip you?'

Peter left. He had better things to do than to stand there listening to Clare hurl insults at him.

Clare continued to hail abuse after him. 'Go on! Go to your whore. I don't want you any more anyway . . . and neither do the children. Get the hell out of here and out of our lives. Do you hear? You're ruined. I'm going to make sure that Daddy hears what you're doing and who you're doing it with. Don't ever come back here, d'you hear me? Don't come back here ever again!' She reached for the last case that Peter hadn't been able to carry. As she hurled it after him it bounced down the steps and cracked open, strewing Peter's clothes all over the garden path.

Clare stood and watched him struggling to gather up his belongings before he threw them on the back seat of his car and sped off through the gates. Only then did the true feelings of pain begin to dawn. Only then did she want him more than she ever had before.

21

Lowestoft Prison, Early April 1985

'I'll fucking kill her!' Perry told his visitor venomously. 'I really can't believe it. She used to be an angel. What made her change? I just can't believe it!' He rubbed his face in total frustration. His visitor had brought him news of Tiffany's plans. As Chantelle's father, Grace felt he had a right to know. 'So, she's away all week and every week, neglecting Chantelle, dating an MP, a married man! I really just cannot believe it. What's wrong with her? It's all my fault, isn't it? If only I hadn't been caught, if only I wasn't stuck in here, if only I'd not asked her to bring in the weed for me. She didn't want to do that, but I went on and on. I forced her to do it and if only I'd . . .'

'Stop blaming yourself and trying to find excuses for her. There was nothing that you could have done to stop her doing what she's been doing,' Grace interrupted. 'I know that you did your best for her, she told me that. She told me everything, about the way that you helped her when she was really down, gave her a home, gave her all that you could. And you loved her, didn't you?'

'Yes, I did.'

'And didn't she say that she loved you, that she would wait for you?'

'Yup.'

'So the very least you would have expected was for her to wait for you and support you on your release?'

'That's the way that I saw it, but Tiffany doesn't see it like that, does she? And it's been so long. Was I expecting too much, asking her to wait for seven years?'

'In my opinion, no. I've been without a partner now for longer than that so it can be done. She's the one who's being selfish and the more I think about it, d'you know what? She used you – and now that you need her, where is she? In bed with another man and I've even heard Chantelle call him Daddy.'

'God! What a bitch!' Perry slammed his hand down on the table. 'If I ever see her again, she's dead. I swear I'll kill her. I've only got three months to serve but, even if it means coming back in here again, I'll kill her!'

'You know I had to tell you, Perry. I had to bring you up to date because things are getting pretty serious. Do you blame me?'

'Blame you? Blame you for what? You've done me a favour, Grace, and quite clearly you care for her. And you know what, you're just so totally different from how I had imagined you? I'm not quite sure what I expected but, after all Tiffany's told me about you, I wouldn't have expected you to have a heart at all and obviously you've got a big one.'

'Why? What did Tiffany tell you about me?'

'About the rape. That you allowed her to be raped by your boyfriend. You could have done something, you could have stopped it, but you just let it go on.'

'I just can't believe that girl. It doesn't matter how hard I try to help her, how often I forgive her, she always sees me as the enemy and tells people lies about me.'

'So isn't what Tiffany said about the rape true?'

'No, it's not. That little ... I'd been dating this guy called Kevin for about a year and he had asked me to marry him, but because we'd lost our parents and I was the only relative Tiffany had, when I told her what was going to happen she went berserk. She said she was going to make sure that she found a way to stop it, because if I got married, then she'd have no-one ...'

'. . . and for all this time I believed her! You see, if you hadn't come down here, I would still have thought that you were responsible.'

'I haven't finished yet. So she tries to seduce him, right? She figures that if she can get him into bed, then I won't want him any more and our marriage plans will be over. So she tries it on and, being a man, he falls into her trap: she cries rape and the rest you know. And, suffice to say, I didn't get married to him and d'you know what? It's hard for me to say this,' Grace snivelled, 'but, as I told you before, I haven't had a boyfriend in ten years because I just haven't been able to trust another man since.'

'Grace, I'm so sorry. I don't know what to say. So she's effectively ruined your life, not the other way around?'

'Yeah, that's right.'

'I feel so sorry for you.'

'Look, you won't tell her that I came to see you, will you? I'm just so worried about Chantelle; I had to talk to someone and Tiffany's not interested, she's not paying attention to her at all.'

As Grace headed back on the train, she reflected on her afternoon's visit with Perry and felt that it was a job well done. She'd managed to persuade a neighbour to have Chantelle for the day. When Tiffany came back later that evening, flaunting her expensive engagement ring, Grace felt she would just about be able to keep the pangs of jealousy under control knowing she had successfully completed her mission.

'Just three more months.' She wrapped her arms warmly

around her large frame as she snuggled up on the British Rail seat. She thought she'd have a snooze to break up the long journey back to London. She closed her eyes and wondered just what Perry had in store for Tiffany. Yes, today she was very happy. Well, why should Tiffany have all the happiness? For crying out loud, she had *everything* else.

22

Islington,
1985

Marcia couldn't say for sure but it certainly did look like her. But it couldn't be. What would Tiffany Ideh be doing in the foyer of the Hitenhaven Hotel in Brussels? Marcia was inspecting the large picture that had appeared the previous day on the front page of the *Observer*. It featured the man of the moment, Peter Duvall MP, and the story was about his recent fact-finding trip to Brussels. Peter Duvall, loved by everyone, man, woman and journalist. He was always worth a picture and would also be worth a story, if she could ever get to him, but no matter how closely she examined the photograph, turning it upside down, squinting at it from every angle, she just couldn't be sure. Tiffany, if it was her, was out of focus anyway since she hadn't been the one the photographer wanted. And what would Tiffany Ideh be doing in Brussels? It wasn't as if it was the fashion capital of the world and, anyway, she'd stopped modelling months ago for some unknown reason. It was curious because Marcia could remember that she had just started to do very well. If she had kept going, she would have been mega by now.

Entertainment being Marcia's arena, she knew all that there was to know about stars and who was up and coming. It was a natural skill of hers to spot them before they broke. That was why she had noticed someone who just might be Tiffany Ideh in the background of a photograph of Peter Duvall when the photographer from the *Observer* probably hadn't even realised what he'd got. That was what a scoop was all about and, knowing that scoops make big bucks, that was what Marcia was all about. She'd had enough of scrimping and scraping. If she saw something that she liked in a shop, she wanted to be able to buy it there and then. Instead she was always broke and drove a six-year-old Ford Fiesta badly in need of a mechanic. She doubted whether it would even pass its MOT, which was due in a couple of months time.

'It's Patrick for you,' Greg shouted and Marcia picked up the telephone on her desk.

'Hi. How are you? Are you missing me?'

'Yeah, of course I am. That's why I'm phoning you from the staff room between lessons to say hi.'

'Well, hi.'

'Hi.'

'Are you gong to pick me up tonight? Do you fancy going out?'

'Oh, honey. I've got so much marking to do. Can we leave going out till the weekend?'

'Sure.'

'OK, I'll come round and do my work at your flat and then we can keep each other company. About seven-thirty?'

'That's fine.'

'OK, see you then, honey. Bye.'

'Bye, my sweet.'

When Marcia hung up, she pretended to put a finger down her throat to indicate how sickened she was by the conversation. Patrick was only thirty-one, but he carried on like a pensioner. To suggest going out through the week was a crime as far as he was concerned. Couldn't possibly do that. And all of his sweeties and honeys. Please! She wanted a real man. But Patrick had his uses, he bought her things so he would do for the time being. Right now she didn't have the time to find someone else.

Philip Grange walked into the office. He was one of two white people employed at *Your Choice*. Two cameras hung round his neck.

'Wow! You look like death warmed up,' said Marcia. 'How come you look so rough?'

'Remind me to pay you a compliment some day.'

'Oh, I'm sorry, Philip, I didn't mean to be rude or anything, but although you're always in jeans you're usually one of the smarter photographers. And certainly the best-looking,' she added with a flirtatious grin.

He smiled. Marcia was undoubtedly the prettiest woman in the office and it was always nice when she paid attention to you.

'I've been away this weekend. I covered the Gregory Isaacs concert in Amsterdam and then as soon as I flew in yesterday I had to catch a train from Heathrow all the way to Cockfosters for a gay rally, and that went on all night. I haven't slept yet and I feel like I've been from one end of Europe to the other. I only came in to drop this film off and I'm off now too.' He went out of the door, only to return seconds later. 'Marcia, guess who I saw at Heathrow yesterday. She'd just come off the flight from Brussels.'

'Don't tell me. Let me guess. Umm, umm, Tiffany Ideh? Right?'

'How in heaven's name did you guess that? She hasn't been around for ages. How did you know? Well, spoil my surprises then, I don't care.'

'So it *is* her in the picture.' Marcia picked up the paper again. What on earth was Tiffany Ideh doing in Brussels with Peter Duvall?

Marcia had been with *Your Choice* now for far longer than she had anticipated. It was time to move up on to a national newspaper but, try as she might, her job applications were turned down and she was becoming disillusioned. It shouldn't be the colour of your skin that mattered, just the standard and quality of your work, but the day that turned out to be the case would be a day of dawning for every black person in the whole wide world.

At least her editor, Vaz Littleford, had recently allowed her to specialise in the area where her real interests lay. All that she needed now was to find something that no-one else had to distinguish her from all of the other equally talented writers. What she needed was a scoop, and Marcia was a real journalist through and through. She had a sneaking feeling about this one. Yes, it was a wild guess, but what did she have to lose? She felt overcooked at *Your Choice* and was ready to move on to another league. She needed a break. Would she find it in a story about Peter Duvall and Tiffany Ideh?

23

Kent, 1985

Peter's next stop after leaving Clare was to be the House of Commons and he knew that was going to be just as hard as dealing with his wife. He needed to hear Tiffany's voice to give him the courage to go through with it.

'Hi. It's me. Is Tiffany there, Grace?'

Peter Duvall, she guessed. Couldn't he even let half a day go by without calling? Tiffany was out. She'd said that she wanted to buy something new to wear for the dinner she had been going on about ever since she got back yesterday, the one where she was going to introduce Chantelle to the man who she believed she was going to marry.

Grace's meeting with Perry had been very rewarding. Perry was going to visit her as soon as he was free and then Tiffany's relationship with Peter Duvall would be history. But that wouldn't be for another three months and here was Peter on the phone again. Grace felt the old bitterness and resentment surge through her. How on earth did her sister get a man like Peter Duvall, a fucking Government minister, to fall for her like that? Quite clearly he adored

Tiffany and Grace was in no doubt as to how Tiffany felt for him: there wasn't a conversation in which his name didn't feature. If possible, Grace would rather not wait another three months to see whether Perry could put a stop to Tiffany's plans. With Tiffany out, maybe Grace could try to do something about it now? Quickly, she improvised.

'Oh, is that Perry? Perry, Tiffany's just gone to the shop. I think that that Peter Duvall has given her some money and she's gone to spend it on even more junk.'

Peter hung up. He must have dialled the wrong number. He'd try again.

But once again Grace's voice said, 'Perry? Is that you? What happened to the phone?'

Peter didn't know what to say. He knew that he hadn't got the number wrong this time. He had to find out who Perry was.

'Grace? Is that you?'

'Yes.'

'It's Peter, Peter Duvall. I called just a minute ago. Grace? Don't hang up. Look. I know that you're Tiffany's sister; I know that that is where your loyalty lies given that you're family, but I need you to be straight with me. Grace? Are you still there?'

Grace felt that for once she was going to be able to do something which would have an immediate effect on what she wanted to destroy. She was on a roll now. No way was she going to stop.

'Oh, Peter, I didn't know it was you. I thought that it was Per . . .'

'Perry. You can say his name. I heard you say it before. It's Perry, right?' Grace didn't say anything. 'Grace? If only you knew what I was going through right now. My life is just . . . I don't know what my life is at this moment, especially in light of what you've just said. You've got to talk to me. Please talk to me. You said Perry. Who is he, Grace?'

'Oh, Peter. I'm so sorry. I can't believe that I could have made such a stupid mistake. Please forget what I've just said. Please. Otherwise Tiffany will kill me.'

'Tiffany won't kill you.'

'Of course she will. I would have ruined all of her plans.'

'All of Tiffany's plans? What plans are you talking about, Grace? And you still haven't answered my question. Who's Perry? Are you going to tell me?'

'How can I? Oh, I can't believe that I allowed that to slip.'

'Well, now you have, Grace, and I've got a right to know exactly what you were talking about. Look, did Tiffany tell you that I proposed to her when we were away? . . . Yes, she did tell you, I can remember her saying that she wanted to call you when we were in Brussels. Grace? I know that you made a mistake in thinking that I was Perry, but if this turns out to be anything like what I'm guessing, there won't be any need for you to fear Tiffany because I just won't be around to tell her that you told me. I'm going through major changes in my life right now and . . . Look, Grace. I won't tell Tiffany that you told me, I promise. Just tell me everything so that I can make up my own mind.'

That was all that she wanted to hear. Peter Duvall had given her a green light to go, go, go and that was exactly what she did. She told him that Perry was really Tiffany's fiancé and that he was presently serving a prison sentence for armed robbery and attempted murder. He only had three more months to serve and then he would be coming back to live with her.

'Remember the flat that you offered? That's why she didn't want to move. She didn't want to give up this flat, Perry's flat, to go to live in yours, when she knew that he was coming out and that was who she was going to be with.' That made sense to Peter and so did the tales of how Tiffany had only planned to use him. Her plan must have been to get as much money out of him as possible so she could set things up for her and Perry. He realised that was why Tiffany hadn't been really pushy about them getting married, moving in together or going out in public together. But then came the biggest blow of all.

'Peter, I really didn't want to tell you any of this, but I have to agree with you. You have got the right to know what's going on because it affects you, too. Like you said, Tiffany is my sister and that is where my loyalty lies, but I can't stand by and watch her doing something wrong without saying anything, especially when it's hurting someone else.'

'Go on, Grace,' Peter encouraged gently.

'Did she tell you about Chantelle?'

'Chantelle? Chantelle? No, I don't think that I've heard her mention that name, but she might have.'

'Umm, no. Umm, I think that if Tiffany had mentioned her name, you would have remembered.'

'Chantelle? Why?'

For effect, she waited a few beats before revealing, 'Because Chantelle is Tiffany's six-year-old daughter.'

'What! You've got to be kidding me?'

'Nope.'

'Grace, I just can't . . . I just can't . . .'

'I know how you must feel . . .'

'No! You don't.'

'Yes, I do, Peter, because I've shared in the sorrow of the men she has done this to before. Believe me, I do know how you feel.'

'You've got no fucking idea how I feel. No fucking idea at all!' And he slammed down the phone.

The timing was perfect. Just as she put the phone down Tiffany waltzed in, laden with shopping bags.

'Look at this, Grace. When I walked past Evans it was on a dummy in the shop window. It was really expensive but

I thought, that would look great on my sister. Here, Grace. Why don't you see if it fits?'

Tiffany handed her the bag. Grace wondered if Tiffany would ever learn not to be such a nice, considerate person. Anyway, what did she need yet another outfit from her sister for? She never went anywhere.

Grace tried on the trouser suit.

'It looks lovely, it really does. Listen, are you going to pick Chantelle up today?'

'That's a strange question. Of course I am. Why?'

'Oh, only because I'm in for the whole day today and I could have done it. Anyway, I wouldn't mind going to bed again. This shopping has really tired me out. I'm going to go and lie down again, OK? Peter's going to be here at seven. Can you wake me at five so that I can grab a shower and give Chantelle a bath before he gets here?'

24

Kent, 1985

Peter left the callbox and sat in his car feeling numb. Wet leaves, blown by the wind, slapped on to his windscreen. They seemed to want to hold on but were flushed away again by the rain. 'I wish that you could do that for me,' Peter thought. 'Wipe away this day in my life.' He wanted someone to tell him what to do, how to handle what he had just been told, but there was no-one he could share this with. His best friend and confidant was Clare's father. How could he possibly go and talk to him?

Peter knew he had to snap out of it. He couldn't sit around in a car park like this for long. There was a car approaching behind him. It might be one of his constituents. Someone might recognise him, start asking questions. Why did I have to chose a woman like Tiffany? he asked himself. She knew what he was doing that day yet she was going to just sit back, waiting for him to ruin his relationship with his wife and end his career. She knew that he was doing all of this for her. How could she have treated him like that? He'd put everyone above her, his wife, his children, even his job, and this was how she was going to repay him?

Why hadn't she even mentioned that she had a child? Had it been her plan from day one to use him? God! When he thought of what might have been had he not stopped off to call her. He would have handed in his resignation! And for what? Nothing!

Grace had obviously done him a great service, but if he had known earlier he wouldn't have told Clare about Tiffany. He would most probably have just left her, or maybe he would have continued in their farce of a marriage until someone else came along. No, he still felt good about leaving. His marriage was over: there was no going back with Clare.

Peter decided the only thing to do was to go away for a while to give his bruised ego time to heal. But before he did anything else, he had to to see Clare again. He'd tell her to give him a week and not to talk to anyone, especially her father, about what had happened, before he came back. He knew that she loved him. She would do that for him.

This was the best way to handle things. The only way. Just take control of his life again.

25

Ealing,
1985

When Peter didn't turn up at seven o'clock to take Tiffany to dinner, Grace didn't say a word.

'It's so unlike him to do that. Not even a call.'

Grace still said nothing.

'Something must have gone wrong at home when he spoke to his wife. That's what it is. I'm sure he'll call later, or tomorrow.'

Tiffany put Chantelle to bed but she couldn't sleep herself. She had to admit that she was very worried that maybe Clare had convinced him to stay. Maybe she had something over him which would force him to stay? Maybe he no longer wanted to leave? Maybe it had all been one elaborate hoax in the first place, just to see how gullible she really was? There were so many maybes.

But when she called him the next day she was told he had gone away. She would have to wait a whole week before she could reach him. They had always agreed that she would never, ever call him. And thus far she had never needed to, he had always called her. Now, in agony through worrying about why she hadn't heard from him, Tiffany pretended to be somebody else and was finally put through to Peter.

She had suspected something must be wrong but it still came as a devastating shock when he told her the engagement was off.

'You can keep the ring. Pawn it,' he barked, 'and then you can use the money for Perry.'

'Perry? You know about Perry?'

Although he was stronger than the day when he heard the news, her voice still made him ache. He had wanted what Grace told him to be wrong, but clearly Perry was part of her life. He had held out a little hope that the information he had might be wrong and they could get back together, but now that hope had been dashed.

'Who told you about Perry?' she asked.

He'd already thought about what he was going to say in response to that question.

'Don't forget what I do for a living. I'm a Government minister, although you tried to wreck that, but I've still got friends in the Home Office. I can find out anything about anyone and, by the way, how's Chantelle?' There was a stunned silence on the other end of the line. 'Yes, Tiffany. I know about her too. How could you? Didn't anything that I said, or anything that I did, mean something to you?'

There was a knock on his office door.

'Peter, can't we meet and talk? Last Monday, when you didn't turn up, I swear that I was going to tell you everything. You've got to believe me.'

'I've got to do what?'

'You've got to believe that I was going to tell you. I love you, Peter, and you haven't even given me the opportunity to explain.'

'Because I don't want to hear your explanations and your excuses. It's over between us. It's finished.'

'I can't believe that you're doing this, not even a phone call. Nothing.'

'I think that if you look at your relationship carefully, you'll be able to see that it's not me who owes you, sweetheart, it's the other way around!'

There it was. She'd wondered when it was going to come. Just like Perry, he hadn't given her anything out of real love. What was it now? Pay-back time? And why had he mentioned Perry? So what if her ex was in prison? It didn't make her a bad person.

'So what do you want me to do now, Peter?'

A knock sounded again. His secretary was under strict instructions not to enter until she heard him say so.

'I want you to leave me alone. I'm aware that you've been calling. The fact of the matter is that I only got back to the office today because I've been away. But don't phone me again. I don't want to hear from you. Just leave me alone.'

'Can't we at least talk? Christ, Peter, you can't just end it like this.'

'Watch me!' were the last words she heard him shout.

Grace had picked up the extension late and only managed to listen to half of their conversation. She hung up and walked into Tiffany's bedroom.

'I can't believe that he didn't even call. It doesn't make any sense. No sense at all,' Tiffany told Grace. 'Hey, on the night that Peter was supposed to pick us up, remember, when I decided to go back to bed through the day? Did he call here?'

'If he called, I would have told you. Why? Did he say that he called?'

'No. It's just that . . .'

'What? What else did he say?'

'That it's all over. It's all over, Grace, and there's nothing I can do about it.'

'Did he say why?'

'He said that he'd got someone from the Home Office to

do a search on me or something. He also mentioned Perry, but I've got no idea why.' Tiffany started to cry.

'Look, you probably won't believe me right now, but it really is for the best, Tiff. Everything happens for a reason. I mean look at his attitude, he knew he was supposed to be meeting Chantelle that night. How could he have let her down like that? I mean, he did know, didn't he? Didn't he, Tiffany? Didn't you tell him?'

'No.'

'What do you mean, no? Are you trying to say that you've never told him about Chantelle?'

'No.'

'Why didn't you tell him? We talked about it. I don't understand.'

'Right now, Grace, nor do I,' Tiffany managed before breaking down and running out to the bathroom.

And I can't help you with that answer, either, but I am so glad that you didn't, Grace gloated secretly. She'd done a real good job.

It was amazing just how much of her life Peter must have taken up. Now that he had gone, her days seemed so very long and lonely. She'd given up working to please Peter and, even though she contacted Top Ones agency again, they weren't interested in taking her back. In leaving the way that she did, failing to honour the bookings that she had, she'd upset a few clients and that in turn had upset the head booker, Stella Nugent. Tiffany wasn't successful enough for them to put up with that sort of unprofessionalism. To Top Ones, Tiffany was yesterday's news . . . but not to everyone.

A few days after that final phone call with Peter, Grace, who was eager to get her sister out of the flat, gave her a message that a reporter from *Your Choice* wanted to interview her. It was for a feature on the modelling business.

'I've left her name and number on the phone pad,' Grace told her, but for a while there it stayed.

For more than a week Tiffany felt really down, hardly coming out of her room, never going out, but then one day something happened. Chantelle wandered into her bedroom to ask her mum if she would come to watch her in the school play. Tiffany stared at Chantelle and all she saw was an obstacle to her happiness, an obstacle that had blighted her entire future. 'It's all your fault!' she screamed at Chantelle. 'Get out of here!'

As Chantelle fled from the room hollering, something clicked in Tiffany's mind. How could she have done that to such a precious, innocent child? At one time she would never have gone an hour without hugging her daughter, but over the past eighteen months she had let weeks go by without even talking to her. It wasn't just her own life she'd been messing up. She'd neglected her responsibilities as a mother and compensated for her absence with presents. And to think she'd set out to be the best mother in the world!

Tiffany called her daughter back into her room and hugged her tightly. That night, Chantelle slept in her mum's bed and the next day she told Grace that she had been praying to God for that to happen and now he had answered her prayers. Chantelle swore to herself that she was going to start behaving herself at school. She was going to be a good girl.

Now Grace was really worried. For some time now she had been working with Chantelle's school to have her transferred to a boarding school for disturbed children. Chantelle's dreadful behaviour at school as a result of her missing her mother had convinced them that this was the best route to take and Grace, acting as her guardian, had been the person they consulted and whose permission they sought. It had all been about to happen but now Tiffany was spending more and more time with her daughter at home. It couldn't be that much longer before the school heard back from the authorities about their application. How on earth was Grace going to ensure she was sent away if Chantelle and her mother were always together?

Grace tried to persuade Tiffany to have another go at modelling but Tiffany explained that she simply wasn't interested any more. Being a model, if she was totally honest, was so bloody boring. But at least out of all this mess there had come some good. She had realised that there was something much more important and much more special than any modelling assignment, and that was her daughter. That's what she was going to be concentrating on from now and as for *Your Choice*, that wouldn't take long. She'd call them today.

The reporter who had rung for the interview was called Marcia Abiola and she made an appointment to come round and see Tiffany at eight o'clock that evening.

26

Ealing,
1985

'I'm just going out shopping but I'll be back in time so I'll pick Chantelle up today,' Tiffany told Grace.

'But I've told you before, Tiffany. I gave up work to look after her. It's not really fair that, because you're not working and your affair with Peter Duvall is over, you think you can just step in and take over my role.'

'You've been saying that for ages and, while I agreed with it for a while, I think things are a little different now. After all, Chantelle is my daughter, not yours, and I want to look after her. I'm sorry.'

'What do you mean, you're sorry? So what are you saying exactly?'

Tiffany laughed in astonishment. What was wrong with Grace? Why couldn't she grasp it? Chantelle wasn't her daughter. She'd try again.

'I'm saying that I'm really grateful for all the help that you've given me. The past year has been amazing, almost like a whirlwind dream. Sometimes I still can't believe that I was part of it, but it's over now and I've got to concentrate on rebuilding what I shouldn't have let slip in the first place. I'm sure that you can understand that?'

If she could just buy a couple more weeks, Grace fretted, then Chantelle would be off to boarding school, but what would happen if Tiffany went to the school before things were finalised? Perry was coming out soon and then he'd deal with Tiffany and with Chantelle gone, finally Tiffany, like Grace herself, would have no-one; she'd be all on her own. Why did that thought fill Grace with such glee? Anyway, who did Tiffany think she was, trying to take over so late in the game? Everything was set, but if Tiffany intervened now . . . Christ!

'OK. So Chantelle's your child, but she's got used to me doing things for her now. Just give me, say, two weeks before you take over.'

'No!' came the sharp reply.

'I didn't realise it meant that much to her,' Tiffany cried out in despair when she came home later that day to discover Grace's room bare and all her things gone. They had just found each other, she didn't want to lose her sister over this. She rushed to the phone to tell Grace that she would just pick Chantelle up today because it was a bit late for her to get back to Ealing from Brixton now, but that Grace could continue to collect Chantelle from tomorrow. Grace's friendship meant so much to her and she loved her. She'd tell her that. In fact, after picking Chantelle up, Tiffany could then pick Grace up and bring her back home. Why wait until tomorrow when things could be back to normal today?

But when Tiffany dialled Grace's number all she heard was the disconnection tone.

It had started to rain heavily and on such days children had to remain in the school hall until they were collected.

'Mrs Ideh?'

'It's "Miss" actually.' Tiffany wasn't in the mood for ancient attitudes. 'You can have a child and not be married,' she explained to the Head, Mrs Taylor, who had called out to her. Mrs Taylor almost left it. From what she had just heard, and this mother's past record with answering letters and attending meetings, was there any point in trying to talk to her? But she decided to make the effort. For once, this was good news about Chantelle.

'I do beg your pardon. Miss Ideh, do you have a minute?'

'Well actually I'm in a great rush. I've got to go to south London.'

'It's about your daughter, Miss Ideh. It will only take a minute. It's not more bad news, don't worry.'

'What do you mean, more bad news?'

'No, good news this time, Miss Ideh,' Mrs Taylor continued as she led Tiffany into her office and she neatly gathered her skirt beneath her before sitting down, gesturing to Tiffany to sit opposite her.

'But I didn't know that there was ever any bad news,' Tiffany protested.

Mrs Taylor ignored her; she'd obviously misheard.

'There's been such a dramatic change in Chantelle's behaviour and attitude this week. All of the teachers have noticed it and I've asked the Education Board to suspend my application for the special boarding school.'

'What boarding school? What are you talking about?'

'I've asked them to suspend it. We'll give it another month and see how it goes, Miss Ideh.' Mrs Taylor stood up to show Tiffany the door, shake her hand and bid her farewell. She'd said what she had to say. Most schools wouldn't have bothered. With 300 pupils to cope with, she'd already devoted too much time to Chantelle, and her mother didn't even look remotely appreciative. 'I'll put it in writing to you, Miss Ideh, so that you can have a copy of this, too.'

'A copy of this *too*? So you sent me other letters? Look, Mrs Taylor, sit down, please – and start at the beginning. I'm well and truly lost.'

Was it really possible? There had to have been some kind of mistake, but how could that be when she had the evidence spread out in front of her on the sitting-room floor, forty-two letters in total, including copies of letters that she was supposed to have written to the school saying that Grace was now acting as Chantelle's legal guardian. The fact that Grace had been collecting her every day for well over a year had only served to convince the school of her position as guardian. Tiffany couldn't believe it. Could her own sister really be such an evil bitch?

Tiffany didn't drink but she'd seen the comfort alcohol had brought Grace and the way it had made Peter relax. With Chantelle in bed, why not? She fetched a glass and a bottle of Scotch that Grace had left and proceeded to try to drown her sorrows. But she couldn't handle it and she was vomiting in the toilet when she heard the doorbell ring.

27

Ealing,
Late April 1985

'Hi, Marcia Abiola. Pleased to meet you, Tiffany.'

'I'm really sorry you had to wait. I totally forgot that you were coming and the place looked like a war zone.'

Tiffany had rushed to slap her face with water and rinse out her mouth when she heard the doorbell. Now, as she shook hands, she offered, 'Would you like a drink?'

'Yes, thanks. I'll have whatever you're having.'

'Well, I'm not a drinker myself.'

'Nor me.'

'Two orange juices, then?'

'That'll be fine. Thanks.'

Once they were settled, Marcia began to fire her questions.

'What would you say a role-model was?'

'Well, essentially, I think that it's someone who leads by good example.'

'Would you say that you were a role-model?'

'Umm, it depends who . . . Hold on a minute, I thought that this interview was about the modelling industry?' Tiffany thought about her romance with Peter Duvall and

174

keeping Chantelle, her own flesh and blood, a secret. How could she possibly be a good role-model after that? She'd rather not answer that question. 'I really don't want to get into defining what a role-model is or isn't, thanks.'

'Right, yes. OK. How far would you have gone in order to be successful?'

'What do you mean, "how far"?'

'Would you have done anything in order to have been successful in your chosen profession?'

'In my case that didn't arise. It was a fluke as to how I got my start. I didn't have to do anything.'

'Do you think that's fair?'

'Of course it's fair. I didn't set the rules.'

'And how long did it take you to become successful?'

'I wasn't really paying attention to that.'

'Really? Because as I remember, you were working fairly steadily but then all of a sudden you left the profession. Why? When things were going so well?'

What should I do, wondered Tiffany, should I tell her the real reason? She didn't see why not, she'd just not mention any names.

'Well, I was having a relationship with someone who didn't like the idea of me modelling and, since a relationship to me is about listening and respecting your partner's views and I didn't really like what I was doing anyway, I gave it up.'

'I hope you don't mind me asking. Was your partner white?'

'Yes, as a matter of fact, he was.'

'Right. So what do you think about the fact that a lot of successful black people are in relationships with white people?'

Here we go, thought Tiffany, I walked straight into that one.

'I don't really think that you can call me a success any more, but personally I think that love is colour-blind.'

'But isn't love something that grows, unless you fell in love at first sight?'

'No, I didn't.'

'So would you encourage anyone to go that route? I mean, does having a white partner equal success?'

Can you believe this woman, Tiffany thought. What was she really trying to get at? After all that had come to light about Grace and Chantelle that day, Tiffany didn't think she could handle too much more of this crap.

'I don't believe that you should use anyone, black or white, to get where you want to go.'

Marcia expressed surprise.

'But you have to use people, don't you, to get going, at least? I mean, wouldn't you agree that the more influential people you know, the higher you can climb?'

'You're not relating that to me?'

'Is it what you do, or who you know, that separates someone from the crowd?'

'Does it have to be one or the other?'

'You tell me your opinion.'

'You've got a lot of balls, haven't you? You just come right out and ask whatever you want.'

'I don't believe that there's any other way. You've just got to go for whatever you want.'

'Mmm. But it's all mixed up. What are you fishing for?'

'A story. A story on you.'

'Now that could be dangerous.'

'For whom?'

'Whoever.'

'Well?' Marcia persisted.

'Well what?'

'Is it what you do or who you know? Which would give you the highest climb?'

'I can't answer that. All that I know is that however you get there, the higher you climb, the further there is for you to fall.'

'That's good. I'll remember that.'

At one stage Tiffany thought that Marcia must have been sent to annoy her and that there was probably a photographer lurking about outside, ready to snap her brutally throwing the reporter out. But after the so-called interview they sat and chatted for ages, supposedly off the record.

Marcia might be a go-getter but she was actually very nice with it.

'I pity anyone who gets in your way,' Tiffany joked, and they both laughed. But later it would prove not to be so funny.

Tiffany was careful to skirt around her life history, aware that while Marcia seemed incredibly friendly, she was first and foremost a hungry reporter. At around eleven o'clock, Tiffany told her that she had to kick her out. She needed to get some sleep because her sister had hit her with a major problem earlier that day, and as a result her brain was so tired it was about to shut down.

'Do you want to talk about it, definitely off the record?'

'Maybe some other time but not tonight. I really have enjoyed meeting you, though.'

'Likewise,' Marcia said, although her attitude to this new friendship was based on a different agenda altogether. She could smell a scoop in the wind, sense a certain naivety in Tiffany, and a vulnerability. She was sure there was a story here, a major one. A friendship with Tiffany would mean that she would be on the pulse when it broke. She didn't want to ask her outright about Peter Duvall. She didn't want to put her on her guard or for her to alert Peter that someone knew. She'd keep cool about it for the time being.

'What about going out for a drink tomorrow?'

'But we don't drink.'

'That's true. A meal, then?'

Tiffany hesitated for a second. She hadn't forged many

friendships, always preferring to keep herself to herself, but in the past few hours she'd felt that Marcia could well be the friend she was looking for. She needed someone to share things with and even after their short meeting, she felt an affinity with her.

'Yeah, OK. I'll get a babysitter for Chantelle.'

'How old is she? Six, right? Bring her with us.'

'Yeah. OK. I'll do that.'

'I'll meet you here, shall I, at say, six-thirty?'

'That would be fine.'

And so the 'friendship' began.

28

Brixton,
May 1985

Tiffany thought better of visiting Grace the next day. She was boiling over with anger and she didn't want to meet her sister feeling as she did. She'd leave it for a while and maybe Grace would contact her.

A week later, Tiffany arrived at seventeen Graford Tower in Brixton just after ten in the morning. She'd thought that her estate was bad but this really was the pits. No wonder Grace had been in such a hurry to move in with her. In the week that had passed since her rapid departure, she had not called to offer an explanation, no apology, nothing.

There was no answer to her knock. She deliberated whether or not to use the spare key Grace had given her but decided to wait. It was only when she saw the postman delivering the second post that she decided to go into action. If Grace could intercept Tiffany's letters about Chantelle, why shouldn't Tiffany respond in kind? She got out of her car, let herself in to Grace's flat and picked up the mail from the doormat.

'... Thanks for keeping me up to date on everything,

Grace,' Perry's letter read. 'I can't believe that she threw you out when you suggested that she should end her relationship with big shot Peter Duvall because I was coming out soon. And I bet that you're right about him only using her. White men always have sexual fantasies about black women.

'I'm finding it so hard to come to terms with the change in Tiffany but it won't be long now. Soon I'll be able to see for myself. I've spent my weekend leaves here in Suffolk because I wasn't ready to face her, but now I really am. Thanks as well for the invitation to stay with you until I get myself sorted out. I've got to go and see some people first so I'll make my own way and I'll see you on July twenty-fourth at about nine pm.'

Tiffany opened another letter from the Department of Social Security instructing Grace of their decision to deny her unemployment benefit because their enquiries revealed that she had been sacked from her last job and therefore she didn't qualify.

'Oh, God. She must be unstable. There's no other explanation. She's been telling me lie after lie. And I dread even to think what she was fired for.'

Grace was out to get her. Not long ago Tiffany had had a lover, a sister and a luxurious lifestyle. Could it have been jealousy that made Grace do all of these terrible things to her? Well, maybe Grace would be happy now. Everything was gone – all that was left was a nightmare.

'I love you, too,' said the voice-over as THE END appeared in block capitals and the credits began to roll on the television screen.

'Oh, what a happy ending,' said Marcia as she rose from her seat, yawned and stretched. 'How sweet.'

'It's a load of crap!' snapped Tiffany. 'Whose bloody life is like that? I do wish they'd start reflecting the real world!' She mimicked the actress's last words, 'I love you, too . . .

Utter crap! And did you see that ring he gave her? Now come on. How many council tenants have had one of those given to them?'

'You have.'

'How'd you know that . . . ?' Tiffany looked down at her finger which still sported the ring that Peter had given her. She was no fool. Unlike some other women, no way was she giving it back.

'Well, that's different. I mean, how many more do you know? . . . See?'

'Oh, here we go again.'

'What do you mean, here we go again? Well, how many *do* you know then? Why is it that they keep depicting good looks, high living and being in love as though they're the be-all and end-all?'

'Maybe because they are? Look, I really don't want to get into this again right now,' Marcia said firmly, raising her hand in a stop signal. She began to gather her belongings from the smoked-glass coffee table – lighter, cigarettes and mints – putting them away in her handbag.

'You're not making any sense. Everything you now resent, you once had. You *were* the person in a magazine, the face on a billboard. All of what you say you hate, beauty and wealth, was yours not long ago, and you were also blissfully in love, weren't you? For the life of me I don't understand it. I mean, isn't that what everyone aims for? And it's stupid you shouting at me for it; I might work in the media but you know that I can't change anything, so why do you keep harping on about it? Hearing these constant complaints from someone like you really doesn't make any sense at all, unless . . . unless of course you decide to make it make sense to me. I mean, for crying out loud, Tiffany, *what happened to you*?!'

Marcia had asked that question a thousand times before and was aware that it was always the cut-off point for Tiffany. 'No! Don't tell me. I really don't want to know any more.' Maybe if she played it this way, acting disinterested, this time Tiffany would go a little further. But she didn't.

Marcia was desperate to know the whole story. She had a burning desire for gossip. It was the root of her work. So when was Tiffany going to reveal the reason why she was so venomously resentful? All that Marcia knew was that it had something to do with her child's father and her sister Grace, but what was it? Marcia knew Tiffany's ritual all too well. She'd see a film, a photograph, anything showing happiness and wealth, and it would send her over the edge. Soon she would start attacking Grace and Perry, but she always knew just when to stop. Marcia had always told her that she was there if she needed someone to talk to (albeit for Marcia's own professional benefit), but she knew she only ever heard as much as Tiffany wanted to tell her.

How could she persuade Tiffany take it one step further? Maybe there wasn't anything else to get anyway? Tiffany might well be aware of all of the curiosity that she was arousing by her tantrums and just be after sympathy. Or of course it could be very simple. She often talked about the restrictions on her freedom and the added responsibility that came with being a single parent. Maybe it was that? Self-pity. Well, even that might make a story:

'Ex-Star Model Unable To Cope With Motherhood!'

Maybe she was penniless or in debt? No. There was something bigger. Much bigger. And Marcia was sure that Peter Duvall was involved somewhere. Well, she'd only known Tiffany a week. They'd seen each other every day since they'd met, but obviously Tiffany wasn't ready yet. Marcia would just have to wait. She was in the best position if anything were to come to light.

'When will they learn?' Tiffany asked, neatly diverting the conversation away from herself.

'Look, that type of film isn't supposed to reflect everybody's life. It's for people to try to lose themselves for a while . . . a dream. It doesn't do any harm.'

'Yes, it does do harm, Marcia. It makes people feel as though they're missing out. It makes them regret, it makes them want and, most importantly, it makes people feel jealous!'

'Yes, but those feelings don't have to be negative. I have those same desires. I've always wanted to be a famous writer of some kind from as far back as I can remember. I want to be successful and I'll do almost anything to achieve it, so films like that, full of glamour and wealth, only inspire me. Those films don't make me jealous, they . . . hold on a minute . . . is that what we're talking about here with you? You feel jealous? Look like I said, they should inspire you if you're after that kind of life again. To most people, it's just a programme on TV. They watch it, admire the clothes, maybe fancy the men, hate the fact that the actresses never have a single spot on their face. Then they get up, turn off the telly and that's it, until the next day when another one comes on. You really shouldn't take it so seriously. Don't get jealous.'

'Look, it's not me who's the jealous one!'

'Well who are you referring to, then?'

Tiffany wanted to scream out Grace's name, but what good would it do? There was nothing to boast about in what Grace had done to her. Nothing at all, so the fewer people who knew the better.

'What I mean is that it's just not fair. Tell me what I've done so wrong to deserve this?'

'Deserve what? You're a single parent, Tiffany, that's all, like so many others living in London. You're just back to living in the real world. And don't ever forget that you brought it all on yourself. You told me that *you* decided to give your lifestyle up. Was that true?'

Marcia had always questioned what Tiffany had confided in her. She said she'd ended her relationship with a wealthy businessman who wanted to marry her, but her reactions didn't tally with giving up that lifestyle by choice.

There were other things that were niggling Marcia about what Tiffany had said. She tried a different route.

'Look, you told me you were raped. You didn't tell me the details but I know there's something you find it hard to cope with. I don't know what it is, but in order for me to understand, to help you, you have to tell me why is it that you take everything so badly? What happened with Perry and your sister? Why do you take everything as though it's a personal snipe at you?'

Tiffany was silent, with the set look on her face that told Marcia she had gone too far.

Marcia sighed and got up to put her coat on.

'Oh, you're not leaving already?'

'Yup, I've got to go now. I'm not getting anywhere here, am I, and I want to cover Miss World tomorrow so I've got to get a good night's sleep. I don't want to be around all those beautiful girls and look like death warmed up myself, do I?' She walked to the front door, saying, 'Give Chantelle a goodnight kiss from me and I'll speak to you tomorrow.'

'But I wanted you to babysit for me, just for an hour.'

'Why do you have to go out so late?' Marcia searched.

'It's to do with my crazy sister and Chantelle's arsehole dad.'

'Every time you talk about them, you curse. You still can't tell me the situation?'

'Sorry, I really can't. Not yet.'

Marcia gave in. She was sure that Tiffany couldn't hold out for much longer and if she kept doing her these favours she'd have to confide in her eventually. 'An hour, you say?'

'Yep. Definitely.'

Tiffany had a little errand to run. On the drive over to Grace's flat she thought about what Marcia had said. She so needed someone to talk to, someone to trust, but it always came back to the same thing: she had to remember Marcia was a journalist before she was a friend. Tiffany knew she had been a trusting innocent for too long. She had been betrayed by her own sister, by Peter Duvall, by Perry. The only person she had left was Chantelle. Here she was all alone, without a real friend or a man in her life, but what did that matter when she had Chantelle tucked up in bed at home? She smiled to herself as she remembered the image of Chantelle as a baby, her tiny hands and the soft gurgling sounds she made. The more she thought about it, the more Tiffany decided that there were many wonderful things in her life. It would make a brilliant story. Wouldn't Marcia just love to know!

Tiffany shook herself and drove a little faster. She had something to do. She arrived at Grace's flat and posted the letters she had taken from Perry and the Department of Social Security back through Grace's letterbox. Now she'd give it a few weeks and visit her again. Maybe around nine o'clock on the twenty-fourth of July.

29

Kent,
1985

It was so weird. In just seven days his life had been turned upside down and inside out; even now he still felt out of it, as if a ton of bricks had been dropped on him from a great height. But he had to go on. He had thought that a new life was about to begin for him, but now he had to make sure he was going to be able to salvage the old. He had to see Clare before she put paid to that.

Well, at least when he called she was willing to listen to what he had to say. It was strange, ringing the bell to his own home, or what had once been his home. He waited patiently for Clare to open the door and this time she was more soberly dressed for the occasion.

He was searching for some sort of sign from her, he wanted to get a sense of what his chances were and what her mood was before he spoke. It could make all the difference to what he said and how he said it. But she didn't let on. She wouldn't even make eye contact. As she opened the door and held it ajar so that he could pass, she kept her gaze on the floor.

She too had had a miserable seven days. She'd thought

that her life was well and truly over when Peter left, but now her heart was full of hope again. It may have only been a few days but it had been horrid. She was tormented by the feeling that she no longer belonged to a man who loved her, the feeling that she had failed in her marriage and the feeling of great dread as she mulled over what people's reactions would be when they found out what had happened.

Every time the phone rang since his departure, she'd snatched it up before it could ring twice. She'd listened without uttering a word. When the person spoke, if it wasn't Peter's voice she activated the answering machine. Until she'd spoken to him, she had to avoid talking to anyone else.

The only person she did speak to was her mother, who already knew that she was facing marital problems. But she didn't confide in her about the latest episode involving Tiffany, and though she sounded down during their conversation it didn't give her mother enough cause for alarm even to ask what the reason was. Clare's mother just said she would be round that evening and added, 'I hope you went to your doctor, dear, like I said, otherwise I'll speak to Daddy and get him to prescribe something to suppress your appetite and I'll bring it with me.'

'No, that won't be necessary. I did go, Mother, and he gave me some tablets.'

'Well, that's good news, dear. You'll be nice and slim and have Peter's attention again before you know it. I'll see you later.'

Clare had indeed been to see Dr Flynn, but not to get slimming tablets. What had happened to her in the last week had made her lose her appetite totally anyway she couldn't remember the last time she had eaten. What she had asked the doctor for were strong sleeping tablets, because she also couldn't remember when she'd last had a good night's sleep.

She'd asked Peter on the phone but he wouldn't tell her what he wanted to talk about. She wanted to get prior knowledge so that there could be no dreadful mistake like last time, but he wouldn't say. Really, she knew deep down that there was no reason for him to be coming round other than to beg for her forgiveness. If he wanted to collect more of his belongings she could easily have sent them to him, he could have used Michael, his solicitor, to talk to her about divorce proceedings, so surely this had to be about getting back together. He was coming round to ask whether he could come back home. This was indeed their home. She hadn't built it up on her own and, even though his job had kept him away from it such a lot, she could not view it as being anything other than theirs.

She watched him pull up in his car at the agreed time of five o'clock. She had expected him to come back with the same three cases he had taken when he had left. She thought that she'd have to put a wash on for his dirty laundry, but since he had come empty-handed she guessed that he was intending to do a great deal of grovelling first.

It was actually a good thing that he didn't have his laundry with him because she knew that it wouldn't be good for their future relationship if she agreed to him coming back straight away. She'd have to make him feel that it really was touch and go.

There were questions to be answered, like how was she ever going to manage to sleep with him again, knowing where his penis had been? That would be difficult, but she would try to come to terms with it tonight when they went to bed. Right now, she was ready to hear exactly how he intended to worm his way back into her life.

They sat in silence for what seemed like forever. He had declined her offer of a drink and that was all that had been uttered between them since he arrived. Clare didn't really mind. She did want to hear what he had to say but just having him back there was good enough for her. He could take as long as he wanted.

Clare looked good, observed Peter, she'd obviously made an effort. She was dressed in a royal blue suit, a colour he loved. She already had something similar in her wardrobe and he had once complimented her on it. He thought about all of this in his weighing up of the situation. She was being very amicable at the moment, quite a change from the hysterical outburst she had displayed the last time he was there. He needed her to be in a good mood for what he wanted. It was over between him and Tiffany; not that he wanted it that way, but the things he had discovered about her had forced his hand. If only Clare knew how much he was hurting right now, she would give in to his every request. He finally broke the stillness around them by asking, 'How are you, Clare? Are you OK now?'

Oh, what a stupid question. Where, oh, where had he learned about tact and diplomacy? Clare wondered.

'What do you think, Peter? Do you think I'm full of life and ready to swing from the chandelier?'

'Well, I don't know what to ask you, then, or what to say.'

'Just say what you came to say, that's all.'

'OK.' Peter took a while to compose himself. 'I came here last week to tell you that our marriage was over and that I had fallen in love with someone. Well, the affair's over now, I've ended it. I won't go into the reasons why, but it's over.'

He waited to see if she had anything to say, but all she wanted was to listen and enjoy the grovelling that he was about to do. She had guessed why he wanted to come and it seemed as if she was right.

'I owe you an apology, Clare. Actually, I know that an apology won't make up for what I did to you, but . . . I don't know what else to say.'

'Just say what you came to say, Peter,' she repeated softly.

'Have you spoken to your father about any of this?'

'Not yet. Why?'

'Well, of course, his reaction would, or could, have an impact on me. It could affect my career.'

'And?'

'And what?'

'What do you mean, and what? What else do you want to say to me? You've said sorry, asked about Father: what else?'

'There wasn't really anything else. I just need to make sure that you're not going to tell him. Especially now that the affair is over, does it make any sense involving him?'

'Don't you have anything else to say? Nothing at all?'

Peter wondered what she could be getting at. What else was he supposed to tell her? He couldn't imagine.

'No,' he replied.

'So this meeting is just about saving your skin? The prospect of me telling Father is what you want to curb, is it?'

'Well, yes.'

'And there's nothing else for us to talk about? You've got nothing to say about our marriage, our children, you and me?'

'I didn't come round to talk about that right now, no, but I understand that you might be eager to put our divorce in motion as soon as possible. Whenever you want to start the proceedings, it's all right with me.'

'But now that your affair is over, do you still want us to get a divorce? Why aren't you asking whether you can come back home?'

'Because my affair didn't cause our marriage to break down; it was the result of it.'

Oh God! He'd made a fool of her once again. Why hadn't she learned the first time? But she couldn't just let it end like this. Whatever it took, she had to get him back. She had already experienced a week living with the knowledge that their marriage might be over. She hadn't liked it one bit and she didn't want to go through one more day. She couldn't.

'Peter, come back home,' she pleaded. 'Even if you don't want us to have a sexual relationship, I can cope with that now, really, I just need you to come home.'

'Clare, I don't understand this come home bit. I was hardly ever here when I was supposed to be here.'

'I don't care about how much time you spend here. I just need to know that I'm not living a lie and that this is your base. Bring your clothes back home. You owe me, Peter. That's all that I ask.'

That's all she was asking? The way she put it it didn't seem like a lot, but really what she was asking for was his life again. He'd just got his freedom back, he'd just managed to walk out of a marriage that was going nowhere; he had no intention of going backwards.

'I can't do what you're asking me to do. Do you understand? I mean, I shouldn't have to remind you that our marriage wasn't working, you were part of it. I'm fed up with living a lie. As for the children, I'll keep providing for them, you know that, but I don't want to move back, Clare. I can't.'

'But that's not what I want. What about *me*?'

'Clare, you have to make a life for yourself. You've been depending on me for everything for so long. It's time to take responsibility. Go and make a life for yourself. Get a job, I don't know, do something.'

'What's that? Some kind of sick joke? Yes, I may have made you my life and yes, I depended on you, but it suited you then, too, you wanted it that way. And now, now that you've used me and you've got no further need for me, you're just tossing me away like old, unwanted furniture.'

'I don't see you like that, Clare. Not at all.'

'So what *do* you see when you look at me?'

'I see the mother of my children. A woman I respect and care about.'

'But not the woman you love?'

'No, Clare. I don't love you. Not any more.'

'Did you ever?'

'What kind of a question is that? I married you, didn't I?'

'But the love that you say you felt for your mistress. Did you once love me like that?'

If he was being honest, he'd have to say no. He'd never felt for Clare the kind of passion with which Tiffany set him alight. Tiffany was like no other woman he had met before or was ever likely to meet again, but he couldn't tell Clare that. He would have to lie.

'Of course I did,' he said finally. But he had taken far too long to answer, and Clare knew he was lying. She'd already thought about her next course of action if he wasn't going to come back home straight away and it seemed as if she would have to put it into gear. Her mother was coming around at nine that night. Clare had anticipated Peter being there too. She had imagined being able to show her mother how well they were getting on and working things out, but now her mother was going to learn the truth, that he was gone. Clare couldn't stand it. She wouldn't let it happen. She'd give it one last stab before she played her ace card.

'What if I said that I would speak to Father and tell him what you've done if you don't come home?'

Peter had had enough. This was outrageous. There was no way he was going to be blackmailed. As long as her father knew nothing about his infidelity, he could proceed with his career without fear of any reprisals from Graham. It was very important that Clare keep her mouth shut about Tiffany. He would come under pressure anyway as a result of the divorce, but that he could face. Graham couldn't insist that he stay with a woman he no longer loved, even if it was his daughter. But he wouldn't put up with blackmail just to keep Graham happy. Clare was going to have to agree to what he had asked with no preconditions. If not, he'd just have to face the music.

When Peter left he had no way of knowing what Clare had decided to do. They'd been talking for an hour and a half and still he was none the wiser. The only thing that remained conclusive was the fact that he wasn't going back there. He made sure she was left in absolutely no doubt about that.

Once again she watched him walk away from her, down the steps, along the path and into his car, but she knew that it wasn't the last time she was going to see him. She had a plan of action that she knew would get him back into their home and back into her life. He'd be leaving her over her dead body!

Her mother was due to arrive, her wonderful, reliable mother, and she had to make the attempt look real. She sat at her desk and wrote what she had to write, making it so convincing she almost believed it herself. Well, that was the whole point. She kissed her babies, knowing it would make her feel as if it were all for real. Although aged eight, seven and five, they were still her babies and no matter what happened between her and Peter they always would be. She felt secure in the knowledge that any day now Peter would be home and they would be able to live a family life again. What Clare had to do she was doing for her babies as much for herself. In a way she had come this far for the sake of the children but now they were no longer enough. Without Peter Clare felt alone, so desperately alone, and she felt like a failure. Jake, Thomas and Sarah had given her so much, but if she didn't take this drastic course of action she would no longer have the strength to give them what they really needed from a mother.

Again she kissed her babies goodnight, she would see them again in the morning and everything would begin to be all right. In answer to their questions, she said that

Daddy had gone an another business trip, but he'd be home soon. She retired to her bedroom and swallowed first fifteen of her sleeping tablets and then another five. That should do the trick, and what did it matter how many she took? Her mother would be there in time to call an ambulance and then she'd be rushed to hospital, Peter would be alerted and he'd definitely stay with her, even if it was out of guilt.

It was funny. Already she was feeling light-headed, as though she was being released from the constant pain she had been suffering. She was doing this for her husband. She was doing this for her children. She was doing it for her marriage. This was the only way forward. This was the only cure.

Five minutes later the phone rang, but neither Clare nor her children heard it. It was Mary, her mother, trying to get through to say that she was going to be late. 'Oh, she's most probably forgotten that I was coming around,' Mary told Graham. 'The answering machine's come on. She's most probably gone out with friends or Peter. I'll just go around in the morning instead.'

30

Cornwall, 1985

As though in celebration of a new dawn the sun was out, proudly shining its brightest rays, when Clare Duvall was slowly lowered into the ground at her private burial. No press were allowed; no unknown intruders wanted.

'Ashes to ashes, dust to dust,' the priest recited as he led the way, letting a handful of earth fall on to the wooden box which encased the corpse. His actions started a procession of similar gestures from the mourners in attendance. Many of them wept as they followed the orator, and in the background was the unrelenting sound, a dull, persistent thud, of earth hitting the lid of the coffin.

Graham, usually the tower of strength for everyone around him, almost collapsed. Then, in a seemingly uncontrollable rage, he began to thump at the ground and with his bare hands started to shovel the dirt on to the coffin.

Peter rushed forward to help him up but Graham just stared at him blankly. Peter stretched out his hand but Graham looked as if he was going to spit at his son-in-law.

'And I encouraged her to marry you! You caused this. You

. . . Just get away from me. I don't want any help from you. I don't ever want to see you again!'

Peter didn't move. He didn't feel that he should have been humiliated like that. All he wanted to do was help. Since Clare's death Graham had cut him off, he hadn't made any contact with him and wouldn't return any of his calls. Well, Peter was hurting too. It had been an enormous shock to him to learn that while he had been talking to Clare on that fated night, she had been plotting to take her own life as soon as he left. He wanted them to all grieve together, comfort each other, support each other, but Graham had clearly shown that he wasn't interested in spending time or exchanging anything but hostile words with him. For the first time in his adult life, Peter began to cry.

Mary hurried to her husband's side and encouraged Peter to walk away to the waiting black limousines that were to escort the family and their closest friends back to Graham's home, away from the tiny village churchyard.

'Just leave it for the time being, Peter,' she said. 'If not for my sake, then for the children's.'

He looked at his children who were standing quietly next to him. Never had Peter felt so alone. Graham, Mary, Jake, Thomas and Sarah were his family, but he felt so detached from them all. His long absences from home while they were growing up meant that he hardly knew his children and they didn't know him. It was to their grandmother, not their father, that they had run earlier in the church, when their mother's coffin lay open for all who wanted to pay their last respects to do so.

As Peter walked away towards the limousines he felt as though he didn't belong there. One day maybe he'd be able to forgive himself for what had happened, but what added to his immense feeling of loneliness was the fact that he could never reveal to anyone what had really taken place between him and Clare. *Never*, unless he wanted to lose his seat and the respect of everyone who knew him. With Tiffany gone and Clare dead he was already an emotional wreck; he couldn't face losing anything else.

He decided that he wouldn't get into the waiting limousine, he would walk to find a taxi. In Clare's suicide note, which didn't mention his affair or Tiffany, she had written about her feeling of failure as a mother and wife since Peter had told her that he didn't love her any more. She wanted her mother to raise her children and she had left instructions that she wished to be buried beside the church she had attended as a child.

Her last requests had been carried out to the letter. Peter was going to give custody of his children to Mary and so now what else did he have? He'd forget about the taxi and just walk, but not to Graham's home. He had the time and he had a lot to think about.

31

Kensington, 1985

Marcia Abiola, now aged twenty-three, looked the spitting image of her mother. She had bold features – high, pronounced cheek bones, large cat-like eyes, short, thick brown hair and, as a result of her mixed-race parentage, an even coffee-coloured skin tone. She was of average build, tall, striking, and she made heads turn. She'd never lost sight of her ambition, but sitting on what she felt was a big story with Tiffany had given her a new surge of get up and go, the will to achieve success; she was striving for that now at any cost.

She had been a journalist for some four years now, for most of that time on *Your Choice*, and she was desperate to crack the mainstream press. Now Vaz had sent her along to cover the Miss World contest at the Albert Hall. She wanted to do it on a bigger scale and had approached every single national newspaper but they were all sending a staff journalist, so she either had to go freelance with it or give her copy to a paper that only sold 30,000 copies a week.

The Albert Hall sat slightly back from the road yet

its bold, architectural structure made it stand *out* as a magnificent building, commanding respect.

'You can't get in there without a pass, love,' said an engineer from the television company that was at the Albert Hall setting up equipment to film the contest live the next day.

'Oh, I don't need one,' said Marcia with more confidence than she felt. She walked towards the back of the Albert Hall where she noticed two more engineers coming out of a side entrance that was wedged open by thick cables running from the television's mobile units into the hall. Looking around to make sure no-one could see her, she slipped in through the open door.

Once inside, Marcia walked around the vast passages. She could hear the voice of Eric Morley bellowing instructions through a microphone and she nipped into one of the many ornate arched alcoves. Marcia looked down on to a vast stage. She counted six cameras and countless leads running from the ceiling to the floor and behind the stage.

Does it really take all of these people to put on one show? she wondered. Tomorrow those same girls down there in jeans, T-shirts and trainers were going to be transformed into stunning beauties, each ready to represent her country, and she was determined to watch how they did it.

After a while she plucked up the courage to move down towards the most beautiful girls in the world who were rehearsing on a catwalk: she braved the walk across the hall to sit among them. It was the ideal place for her to fit in. Her arrival was noticed but everyone just thought that she was another contestant, maybe a late entry. Very soon she was hearing juicy stories about certain contestants and was invited to have her photograph taken, as she didn't have an official badge on display.

'By the way, who are you?' asked one of the chaperones.

'Mary, can you take your girls up for lunch now,' interrupted an organiser.

Phew, saved by the yell as it were, Marcia thought.

Sporting her new identification badge, she joined the girls for lunch where she heard that Miss Spain had lost her wig in the swimming pool while showing off, Miss Ghana and Miss Trinidad were squabbling over the affections of one of the male dancers hired for the show, Miss Brazil may have breast implants and Miss Nigeria was ill and might not be able to take part tomorrow.

'This was obviously meant to be,' thought Marcia, 'the way I got in here so easily, Miss Nigeria being ill and being Nigerian myself; I'm obviously supposed to be in the contest.' Marcia had arrived in the morning and left at about three in the afternoon so as not to overstay her welcome. Anyway, she needed to prepare herself for the next day when she might well be asked to fill in for the ailing Miss Nigeria. On the way out a very anxious Eric Morley asked her where she was going.

'Where's your chaperone? You're not allowed to just wander about like that!'

'Oh, I'm not a contestant, Mr Morley. I'm with the film crew,' she lied. 'Umm, by the way, I am Nigerian and I believe that Miss Nigeria is ill. Any possibility of taking her place if she can't make it? I . . .'

'Absolutely not,' he said firmly and headed off.

'Oh well. How disappointing. I'd convinced myself that it was supposed to happen,' Marcia explained to Tiffany on the telephone that evening. 'I built my hopes up just to let myself come down with an enormous bang.'

'Oh, I know the feeling,' sympathised Tiffany. 'I know it well.'

Vaz Littleford was furious with her and, had she not walked out, he would have sacked her anyway because she covered the show but was only prepared to sell her exclusive behind-the-scenes story to the highest bidder. Vaz felt that loyalty should have prevailed but Marcia told him that loyalty didn't pay her rent, nor did it make her a big name. If she was going to make it, she had to get a move on. It was make or break time.

It was *Goodbye Tales*, a national glossy gossip magazine whose sales were way above any other magazine and still climbing, that bought her story, a bitchy, no-holds-barred look at the Miss World contest. It was *the* magazine to have your work appear in and as a result she was suddenly in demand to cover glamorous events for them and other magazines and newspapers. Marcia's copy was always witty, intelligent and entertaining, and she somehow managed to get just that bit more than other journalists sent to cover the same story. Now that she'd finally been noticed her work won instant acclaim and she began to specialise in what she had always wanted to – entertainment scoops.

Just weeks after the Miss World scoop, Marcia was on a plane bound for Las Vegas. *Goodbye Tales* were sending her there for a heavyweight boxing championship that was being beamed into homes worldwide. Her brief was not to cover the fight but to get a behind-the-scenes story on the champion, Dial Lyson, who throughout his four-year career had never been short of female company. His girlfriends included a number of top black models and actresses. Why had he never married one of them? Was it through choice or was there something else? At twenty-eight, it was time surely for him to settle down. Marcia would find out if there was a story to be told. This was her chance to prove herself once and for all, and she was prepared to do whatever it took to get this story.

Dial won his fight in the second round, one round more than was predicted by the experts, so the early finish was no surprise.

A party was laid on for press straight after the fight where they were allowed to mingle with the returning champion, ask questions and take photographs. Marcia knew that she could get shots from one of the many British photographers there. Armed with her press pass and mini recorder, she made her way to the hotel where the party was to take place wearing full make-up, high-heeled black patent leather shoes and a black PVC dress which revealed more of her body than it covered. She didn't go into the room. How could he possibly see her properly through all his bodyguards, friends and the press? He wouldn't stay in there long, she was sure. How many different ways were there to say how great you felt about retaining your title? And anyway, he was a star and stars didn't stay long even at parties thrown on their behalf.

Marcia decided to wait around in the reception area and sure enough, after twenty minutes Dial was escorted by two bodyguards to the lifts to go up to his suite. He wasn't that tall, maybe five foot ten, but even through his clothes his black body appeared compact and stocky, ready for anything. Marcia caught them as the lift arrived.

'Oh, you're not leaving already?' she purred. 'The taxi that I was in decided to take me on a tour of Las Vegas instead of coming straight here. I've come all the way from London, England and if I don't go back with an interview from you tomorrow, boy, am I in trouble.'

Dial wasn't stupid. He was a sucker for a black chick with an English accent, but he wasn't going to be taken in by that. He was very aware now; he had to be. Previously he'd fallen victim to a female fan who had pretended to be someone that she wasn't. Luckily her parents didn't go ahead with charges or tell the press, even if it wasn't his fault because he had been well and truly duped by her. Since then, he always had women checked out before he dated them, or dealt with them at arm's length and among witnesses. But hey, he'd just won a fight, he'd downed a few glasses of champagne and anyway, Marcia looked far too good to be harmful; he was wondering how she had got into that dress and thinking how he would like to help her get out of it.

'So who do you work for?' he asked as he entered the lift.

'*Goodbye Tales*,' Marcia managed as she reached into her bag to show her press pass. 'You can trust my magazine. You can trust me.'

As the lift door began to close, Dial held it open and extended his arm in invitation.

'Have you had dinner?' he asked in his deep New York accent, speaking with his groin as opposed to his brain.

The story was trailed on TV before it appeared over a period of three weeks in consecutive editions of *Goodbye Tales*.

Week One: 'My Night of Passion with a Twelve-Year-Old.'
Week Two: 'A Congressman Taught Me how to Snort Cocaine.'
Week Three: 'Why My Mum Won't Let Me Marry.'

The editor of *Goodbye Tales* waited for a writ from Dial Lyson's lawyers, but none ever materialised.

'His voice was clearly tape-recorded,' the magazine's lawyers had told them on their several attempts to have the story squashed. 'We're running with it. Sue us if you dare.'

Following just one night of passion, Marcia comprehensively ruined Dial's reputation and career. The congressman mentioned received lots of support from his colleagues but eventually he was forced to resign. In the case of the twelve-year-old, the child's parents who had been paid off at the time decided to break their vow of silence once they learned that they could make a hundred times more for their story than they had been paid. The *National Enquirer* got to them first, though. Dial was eventually stripped of his title and went on to serve a five-year jail sentence for attempted rape.

'It's the nature of my job,' commented Marcia when asked about the effect her story had had on Dial Lyson's life. She had no feelings of guilt about what had happened. 'If he hadn't done anything wrong, I wouldn't have had anything to write,' she rationalised.

While Marcia was away, Tiffany missed her. She was the closest thing she had to a friend now and Marcia would call her daily by phone, but she was still careful to disguise the real reason for her friendship. As it happened Marcia didn't have to wait much longer for her questions about Tiffany's secrets to be answered.

Hot on the heels of the Las Vegas trip came an invitation from the editor of *Goodbye Tales* to interview someone. He'd been offered an exclusive, the first interview with this man since the tragic loss of his wife. He was really excited by the prospect of what the combination of Marcia's writing and the subject matter would do to his circulation. This feature was going to be really hot and Marcia was going to get what she had longed for – an interview with Britain's biggest and best-loved MP, Peter Duvall.

32

Central London, Early July 1985

He paid no attention to her questions about Tiffany and, as for his wife, was it too soon to ask him questions about her death? He'd told her editor that there were no taboo areas, so she'd plunged straight in, asking him outright whether he'd had a friendship with former model Tiffany Ideh. But he wouldn't open up. Something had definitely made him flip. She wondered why he had even bothered to grant them an interview because, apart from staring at her legs, he wasn't co-operating in any way.

Marcia found him so sickening. In the hotel suite booked by *Goodbye Tales* for their interview, his insinuations and gestures had constant sexual overtones. Too many women, female journalists included, had obviously told him how great he was and he'd fallen for it hook, line and sinker. He'd never, ever contemplated the fact that someone might not find him appealing.

Marcia was far from impressed. She could easily do an interview without bringing sex into it. Why couldn't he? How dare he think that glint in his eye would make her swoon? That each touch would have an overwhelming effect on her? If her suspicion was right and he and Tiffany had had an affair, how did Tiffany put up with this arrogant, ignorant arsehole?

She might have slept with Dial Lyson to get a story but, God, at least she'd fancied him. Peter Duvall could forget it. In fact, if he rubbed her back one more time, MP or not, she'd tell him in no uncertain terms that she would rather have sex with a torch.

If Marcia only knew it she'd got the wrong end of the stick. Peter had had enough of women for the time being. Why was this one asking him about Tiffany and how much did she actually know? Women! They always seemed to be around him, constantly letting him down, lying to him, loving him when he didn't want them to, trying to ruin his life, just like this one was obviously planning to do. She was clearly just a bit journalist who was out to make a name for herself. If she knew anything about him and Tiff, he had to stop her spreading such potentially damaging propaganda. He abruptly ended the interview.

Then he complained about her unprofessionalism to *Goodbye Tales*, saying that she had been very disrespectful to him and the memory of his wife. He also lied that she had confided in him her aim to sell her story to *Goodbye Tales'* biggest rival. He knew that would get the editor's goat. The editor knew that was how they'd got Marcia's Miss World story, so there was no need to give her a chance to defend herself. What's more, she'd ruined their scoop. Marcia was told in no uncertain terms that she'd never write for *Goodbye Tales* again, and the word went out in the media world that she was an unreliable, trouble-making journalist, not to be trusted.

What a bastard! Marcia had briefly tasted the success she had craved for years, only to have it destroyed by Peter Duvall. Regardless of his contacts and power, one day she'd make him pay. She hadn't let him know that she actually knew Tiffany, and she certainly wasn't going to mention their interview to her, otherwise Tiffany might become very suspicious as to why Marcia was digging around in her past. Right now Marcia wanted to concentrate on how to get back at this bastard. She couldn't help recalling something Tiffany had said to her: '. . . the higher you climb, the further there is to fall.'

33

Dover,
23 July 1985

It wasn't just that he was lonely, it wasn't just that he had caused his wife's death, it wasn't just that he had been a terrible father sending his kids to live with Clare's mother, it wasn't just that he didn't want even to look at another woman ever again. It wasn't just one thing. *It was the whole fucking lot!!!*

He was standing on the edge of the cliffs in the dead of night. A cool, persistent wind blew, rustling Peter's baggy shirt sleeves as he watched and waited. The night sky was so clear that he felt sure that he could count each and every bright star. Only then did he realise that Clare's action had taken courage. She hadn't taken the easy way out, because right now he had the passion, the reason, the absolute desire to end it all, too, but he couldn't. Clare had taken her life because of him and now he couldn't even pluck up the courage to join her.

He knew he wasn't even avoiding suicide because of the children, although he constantly wondered what they would think of him when, later on in life, they learned the real reason why their mother had left them at such an early age. How could they respect him, how could their love for him last?

Even when he went back and climbed into his car he couldn't bring himself to slip it into first gear, put his foot on the pedal and leave the car to do the rest.

The upper half of his body folded on to the steering wheel where he lay and sobbed. He had to talk to someone, someone who would understand, someone who would listen. But who did he have now? No-one. He knew so many people, but he didn't have any friends. Or did he? He wiped the moisture away from his face with his hand and tried to settle himself – his body, his mind. He knew who to call and as soon as he found a phonebox he would dial her number.

34

Ealing,
24 July 1985

She wondered who was calling her so late at night. It was the early hours of July twenty-fourth. Could it be Perry?

Tiffany hadn't expected ever to hear from Peter again and if she did she had planned to tell him exactly what she thought of him. But when she heard his voice her heart seemed to drop, her anger melted and she just closed her eyes and listened.

She called Marcia and begged her for a favour. She had to go and meet a friend who was in trouble and, although it was one in the morning, could she possibly come over and stay with Chantelle?

'I'm getting a bit fed up with being a good enough friend for you to turn to for help whenever you feel like it, and yet you still shut me out of half your life. I want to help, but I'm also human and I have a healthy human curiosity. I mean, where are you going at this time of the morning?'

'I can't understand why you need to know where I'm going in order for you to do me a favour. Can you come over or not?'

'Are you going to tell me?'

'No. I shouldn't have to tell you where I'm going.'

'You don't *have* to tell me, but you should *want* to; I'm your friend.'

'Friend or not, you . . .'

'What? . . . I what?'

'You've never mentioned it, but I read what you did to Dial Lyson.'

'Dial Lyson wasn't a friend of mine.'

'Look, I just don't want the press snooping around. They're always so busy trying to bring about people's downfall. A friend needs me and he doesn't need press intrusion.'

'What friend could be so important for you to call me at one in the morning?'

'Marcia, I can't tell you.'

'Then I can't help you.'

Marcia hung up, but waited beside the phone because she knew that it would ring again soon. Who else could Tiffany call? She kept away from people, she didn't have any other friends and why should Marcia miss out on this story? If it was Peter, something must have happened. 'Serves the bastard right,' she smirked. But let's hope that he doesn't mention my interview with him – or my name. Marcia felt a momentary pang of nervousness. Nah, why should he? 'Yeah,' she told herself, coming back to life, 'it must be Peter she's going to meet. It sounded serious.'

Marcia had grown to like Tiffany but she had to eat and friendships, like loyalty, weren't going to pay her rent. Anyway, this wasn't about Tiffany any more. She'd get the story any way she could and pay Peter Duvall back for what he had done to her career. And *Goodbye Tales* could also go to hell. She'd do what Peter had said she was going to do and sell her revelations to *Fontale* magazine, their biggest competitor. That would teach them to stick by their journalists next time.

After about three minutes, the phone sounded again.

'OK. But you have to promise me that you won't use it. We're talking about my life, Marcia, and if it involves my life, Chantelle will also be affected. OK?'

'OK, OK. No problem. You have my word.'

Tiffany drew up alongside Peter's car: he had lowered the roof of his Jaguar sports and reclined his seat as low it would go. It had taken her over an hour to drive to Dover and he had fallen asleep by the time she arrived. He didn't hear her climb into the passenger seat and was startled when she woke him.

He held her for what seemed like an hour or more, just held on tight. She said nothing, asked him no questions; he'd talk to her as soon as he was ready. She'd read about Clare's suicide. She'd often been down enough to contemplate suicide herself. But she'd never gone ahead with it and now, being in Peter's arms, she doubted if it would ever cross her mind again.

Because of Clare and the press coverage she'd thought about Peter a lot. But what a day to get a call from him. The very day of Perry's release – how weird the way things worked out. What were Perry and Grace cooking up between them? She hadn't heard from Grace. She would stick to her plan to pay both of them a visit tonight, she hadn't forgotten, but other things had taken priority. She hated seeing Peter like this and knew that she just had to be there for him.

Eventually Peter let it all come pouring out. How bad he felt about Clare's death, their relationship, his children, his whole life. Success had made him become so full of self-importance that he'd forgotten how to be human. He'd wanted to take his own life in order to make a repayment to everyone he'd hurt, but he just couldn't do it. He was a wreck without a direction, a wretch without a reason for living. But since she had come to help him when he called, did he now have a reason for living after all?

They drove to a hotel for the night. Peter needed time to sleep and recuperate and Tiffany needed time to think, not about his question, but about the best way to broach the subject of what he had done to her before. She couldn't just let him get away with it and not say a word. But that could wait.

Tiffany woke early and went downstairs to make a call to Marcia who wasn't terribly happy about being disturbed at six in the morning.

'I think that we should be back in the afternoon, but just in case we're not, can you pick up Chantelle from school as well as taking her this morning?'

'You're taking the piss now, aren't you? What if I had other things to do?'

'Have you?'

'No.'

'Well then?'

'That's not the point. I might have had.'

'If you had, I would have made sure that I got back on time, but since you haven't . . . thanks.'

'This had better be good.'

'What do you mean?'

'There had better be a good reason behind all of this.'

'I'll see you later.'

'About what time?'

'I wouldn't have thought that it would be later than seven.'

They made love when he woke but it wasn't as calm and gentle as usual. There was a great deal of urgency, as if it were their very first time.

He lay on top of her for a while, the white linen sheets loosely draped around his lower half. He'd missed her. He'd missed her sparkle, he'd missed her honesty and he'd certainly missed her body. When she was around he felt as if he didn't have any problems. They all paled into insignificance.

If everything that Grace said was true, then Tiffany had betrayed his trust. But right now he just wanted to enjoy the pleasure of being close to her again, to let his body and mind relax for the first time in weeks. There would be time for questions later.

'I love you, Tiffany.'

'I love you, too, Peter,' she said in reply.

At noon the phone rang in their room waking Peter up. It was reception, informing them that they'd be charged for another day if they hadn't booked out by twelve-thirty at the latest.

'That's really no problem,' said Peter.

Tiffany had eased her body from beneath his and he could hear running water from the shower in the bathroom. He jumped out of bed and decided to join her.

'Where are you going?' she asked as he drew back the curtain.

'I'm going to join you.'

'Here,' Tiffany ordered, handing him her flannel, 'wash my back for me.'

He took the flannel, fully lathered it and rubbed it gently over her back, making it very slippery. He dropped the cloth and began to massage her shoulders, then he kissed the back of her neck and slowly turned her around to face him. He started kissing her forehead, nose, lips, chin and then further down, between her cleavage, her breasts and nipples, and then even further, licking her belly button, the tops of her thighs and around. Tiffany leaned against the cubicle; she wanted to get comfortable for what she knew was about to come. Peter kneeled down, the shower still running, the bathroom filling with hot steam. He lifted one of Tiffany's legs on to his shoulder and grabbed her around her waist for support, then he began gently to nuzzle her vulva, through her pubic hair. He let the slit that he found guide his tongue further inside until he met a hole and slid his tongue as far down into it as it could go, in and out, back to the top of her vulva and back inside again. His hand left her waist and rose higher, finding her nipples which were large and hard. He played with them, held them between his fingers and rubbed them. At the same time he was now paying attention to her clitoris and started to lick around it gently. Tiffany's fingers were running through his hair and occasionally she'd hold his head to guide him in another direction, but then instinctively he'd do what she'd wanted him to do anyway. It felt wonderful. And now he was putting on more pressure and licking her clitoris a little harder. She was about to come and he knew it. As she reached her orgasm, her hold on his hair became tighter and tighter.

When she collapsed in a heap before him he told her, 'Get up. It's my turn now.'

35

Lowestoft,
24 July 1985

'Well you haven't been that bad, not really, actually some
of us will be sorry to see you go, in the nicest possible way,
of course.'

'I suppose that that's the best farewell I'm going to get.
Thanks.'

Perry collected his parcel of clothes and the money he
had accumulated by working over the past seven years. He
was given the time of the next train, his fare for the journey
and a lift to Lowestoft station.

The train didn't go fast enough for Perry. There was so
much for him to do, so many people he wanted to see.
The greenery through his window didn't seem to change
for the whole journey as he passed field after field, but
anything was better than the cream-coloured cell walls that
he had now left far behind him. Tiffany was on his mind
and he still didn't know what he was going to say to her.
He'd never really been a violent type, but he knew that
he wished her harm . . . and a lot of pain.

The train pulled into Liverpool Street station at twelve-
fifteen in the afternoon. The purpose of the weekend

releases he'd had was for him to start to get used to life on the outside, but when you've been away for years nothing can really prepare you.

Perry mingled with the busy commuters as he walked in the direction of the Underground and the Central Line. Things were coming to his attention that previously he'd paid no mind to. The type of suits that the men were wearing, even the colours being worn by conservative types, seemed duller than in the past. He noticed people's shoes and their hair-styles, but the thing that struck him most was that he had never noticed just how noisy London was.

What he saw around him didn't reflect personal wealth, confidence and prosperity. The seventies had obviously been a time for everyone to regress, black and white, and people were darting about as if they had tunnel vision, not communicating with each other. The only ones with smiles on their faces were the models on billboard posters, whose messages were more blatant and sexy than he remembered. As for sex, he needed some, and with a woman. Seven years was a long time to wait. A lot of things had been smuggled into Lowestoft, but no-one had ever managed to get a woman in.

Perry found his way to King's Cross station. He was twenty-eight years old but there were lots of things that he had never done, even before his time behind bars. He'd never bought a condom and he'd never had a prostitute, but there was always a first time for everything.

Perry noticed a chemist across the road from the station and started to make his way over but he didn't get there. A girl blocked his path. 'D'you want some business, mate?'

'Eh?'

'Ten quid, fifteen without a condom, fifteen for a blow job, OK?'

'Yeah, that's fine.'

'Follow me,' she beckoned, walking off in front of him, and he did.

They ended up in a passageway of sheds behind a row of shops near the station. He looked at her vacantly. What was he supposed to do now? How do you start? While he pondered, he could hear another pair getting it together a few sheds down.

'C'mon,' she hurried, pulling him towards an empty shed. 'What's it to be?'

Perry said nothing, but moved towards her as she guided.

'Look, d'yer want it or not?'

He didn't have time to answer. So there is a reason why prostitutes always wear mini-skirts, he realised as she straddled his legs and proceeded to undo his trouser zip.

'You want a fuck, I know you do.'

The word alone was enough. He grabbed at her tits as she bounced up and down and he came. It was over in seconds.

'Fifteen quid,' she said casually, fixing her skirt and chewing gum noisily. She stuck her hand out. He paid her and she was gone.

'Fucking hell,' Perry gasped. 'I need a stiff drink.'

36

Dover,
24 July 1985

They left the Manor Hotel at five o'clock and followed each other back to London where they split up and made a plan to meet for dinner. Peter was to take a taxi and Tiffany was going to drive. They could then go back to Kent and she would have her car there to drive back home the next day.

Tiffany got home just before seven and received a welcome reception from her daughter and an inquisitive look from Marcia. She kissed her daughter and held her hand as they all walked into the sitting room. Chantelle had been reluctant to believe that her mum would get home on time: Tiffany had promised to take her to Pizza Hut that night.

'OK, so what's happened then? Spit it out.'

'It's nothing bad, Marcia.'

'Oh, damn!'

'You should be happy for me, though. I'm going to become Mrs Peter Duvall.'

Marcia screamed with shock. It was just an automatic reaction. Tiffany was going to marry Peter Duvall? Was she serious? What a fucking story! Shit!

Marcia hated Peter. She wanted to be happy for Tiffany but she was too busy trying to tot up in her mind who to take the story to and how much it was worth. This wasn't for a national magazine. This was international news.

She had never in her wildest dreams imagined lucking into a story this big. But if she wanted to get every detail out of Tiffany she'd have to play it as cool as she could, and she'd have to pretend that Tiffany's association with Peter Duvall was news to her.

'Are you talking about Peter Duvall MP?'

'Yep.'

'No wonder you've been so guarded. How come? Where did you meet?'

'Actually, we've been seeing each other for over a year.'

'Well, blow me down. What can I say? Congratulations.'

'Thank you.'

'So? What's the story then?'

'I'll fill you in later.' Tiffany sharply nodded her head in Chantelle's direction. Marcia caught on.

'Well, what do you think about your mum getting married, Chan?'

Chantelle wondered if her mother had even remembered their date. She'd marked it on the calendar that hung on her bedroom wall. It was definitely for tonight.

'It's OK I suppose.'

Chantelle was looking miserable because she suspected she wasn't going to go out with Tiffany, not because Tiffany was getting married.

'Well, don't be too happy for me.' Tiffany hugged her daughter. Chantelle's sulk couldn't dent her happiness. 'You'll grow to love him just as much as I do. You'll see.'

Chantelle doubted that. All she could think of was how last time Peter had been around she hadn't seen anything of her mother and how Aunt Grace had told her that her mum's feelings changed towards her because of this man. She really doubted that she would ever grow to love him.

'Marcia, what are you doing tonight?'

'Oh, here we go again. OK. OK, but I'm going to have to take Chantelle to my house tonight. Patrick's coming over.'

'That's no problem. But you can take her to school in the morning and collect her, can't you?'

'What, from Islington? You're really pushing it . . . Yeah, I'll take her, but when you pick her up I want to hear the *whole* story. Every single detail, right?'

'You've got it.'

Chantelle pushed her bedroom door closed.

Yep. She'd forgotten. She sat on her bed and looked at a photograph of her mother when she was a model. Why was it that her mother was putting everybody before her again? Why was it so easy for her mum to forget about her?

She took the photograph of Tiffany and pressed it against her chest. This way she'd have her mum near her, if only in a picture.

37

London's West End, 24 July 1985

The candle-lit tables in The Elephant on the River gave off a warm, inviting orange glow. Peter clasped her hands in his own.

'Thank you,' he said softly.

'What for?'

'For being there. I don't know what I would have done if you hadn't been on the other end of the phone.'

'I'm sure that you would have done the same for me. Would you?'

He kissed the knuckles of her folded hands. 'I know that I hurt you before. But you have to understand . . .'

'I certainly didn't . . .'

'What?'

'Understand.'

'I know . . . but what you did was serious, though, you must admit that much.'

'Yeah. It was serious and stupid, but I had a good reason, at the time anyway.'

'Oh? What good reason was that?'

'I don't know whether this is a good time to bring this up.'

'Tonight I want everything to come out in the open. It's the only way that we can even think about going forward.'

She wondered if he really meant it. Well, there was only one way to find out. So she began.

'You're in a party that preaches about the scourge of single parents and how they're a drain on society.'

'But that's not aimed at people like you. MPs who talk about those types of issues are referring to people who scrounge off Social Security, not the likes of you.'

'But I've been on Social Security, so it *is* me that they're referring to.'

'It really isn't, Tiffany, because at least you came off it and you started to work and support yourself, but let's say for the sake of argument that they are aiming their words at you, they weren't *my* words, were they?'

'Yes, but they're the words of members of the party you belong to, so in effect you're supporting their views.'

'Do you really think that the whole of the Conservative Party thinks in unison? Agrees on everything?'

'Don't be silly, I'm not saying that, but come on, put yourself in my shoes, when I first met you at that fashion show I was a model, a single parent, black. I know what type of negative connotations there are attached to all those facts, although I don't agree with them myself.'

'But that doesn't make any sense. If you don't agree, why didn't you say something? Why hide it?'

'Because while I don't think there is anything negative about what I am and who I am, some people do.'

'Oh, look, we're going around in circles and it doesn't explain anything. It certainly doesn't explain Perry.'

'What about Perry? I couldn't understand why that would bother you so much.'

'You couldn't understand why Perry would bother me? Are you mad?'

'I must be, because I still don't understand. Is it that,

as your partner, having an ex-boyfriend who has been to jail will be bad for your reputation?'

'Ex-boyfriend. Oh, he's an ex-boyfriend now? When did you split up, last week? Last month?'

'Try eighteen months ago.'

'Yeah, right.'

'What do you mean, yeah, right? Perry and I split up six months before I met you,' Tiffany stated bluntly. 'Surely if your friends from the Home Office can find out that I was seeing him, then they could also find out when I last visited him?'

'Oh!'

'I'm sorry? Is that an apology I heard?'

'Well, it wasn't my fault. That information . . . well, I actually told a little lie about my friends in the Home Office. I didn't get my information from them.'

'Where did you get it from, then?'

'I promised I wouldn't say.'

'But it's incorrect and remember you did say that tonight was the night for us to come totally clean, didn't you?'

'Yes, I did, but I also promised someone that I wouldn't say anything.'

'Oh, come off it. Are you trying to say that Government ministers don't break promises? Come on, Peter, let's not have any secrets.'

'OK . . .'

A waiter arrived at their table and handed them a menu.

'You order,' said Tiffany.

When the waiter had gone Peter cupped and kissed her hands again.

'I don't want us to argue tonight. Let's not waste the short time we have together. We've only got, say, another forty years. Don't let's argue and waste another second.'

'I don't see that what we're doing is arguing, we're

discussing things, things that will affect our future if we don't bring them out into the open now.'

'You're right, of course.'

'Well?'

'Well what?'

'Oh, come on, Peter. You know exactly what I want to know.'

'Who told me, right?'

'That's right.'

'Look, let's get the really important things out of the way, because I still don't understand about your daughter. How could you have denied her existence?'

'I didn't deny her, I just didn't mention her, that's all.'

'But doesn't it boil down to the same thing? You should have told me and given me the choice. It was my prerogative whether I minded or not, and you took that option away from me. It's not as though you've got ten children. You haven't, have you?'

'Don't be silly.'

'Well, if I had minded, all that would have meant was that I wasn't the right man for you, or that I didn't love you enough.'

'Yeah, yeah, yeah. All of that makes sense now, but at the time . . . Do you know what, I even wrote you a song about it?' Tiffany produced the lyrics from her bag and he read them.

'You are crazy. But it does say it all. Why didn't you give it to me then?'

'Because of Grace.'

'Your sister?'

'Yeah. She made me think it was a really stupid idea and I just didn't know how to bring it up after I'd left it for so long. It's like my agent. She didn't even know.'

'How come?'

'Because at the beginning I thought they'd think that

having a child would mean I wouldn't be available to work at short notice or that I wouldn't be able to travel. In fact if it hadn't been for Grace, I wouldn't have been able to do any of the things that I did in the end. And come to think of it, I wouldn't have met you either.'

'You think a lot of your sister, don't you?'

'I did. But . . .'

'I wonder why she didn't tell you that I called that day we were due to meet. In fact she did her best to make me feel really stupid, as though you'd both been laughing at me behind my back.'

'You called? When? Not on the day you were supposed to have picked me up after speaking to your wife? Mind you, that really doesn't surprise me. What did she say to you?'

'I can't remember word for word, but something like,' Peter put on a mock female tone and pursed his lips, 'Perry? Perry, is that you? and, Oh, didn't she tell you about Chantelle, oh dear, and after *all* this time, I thought that she was serious about you. And she said that you and Perry were just out to rob me.'

'She said that?'

'Yes, she did.'

'This is just incredible. I can't believe this. So she's the one who told you about Perry and Chantelle? Man oh man!' Tiffany's smile vanished. 'I just can't leave it any longer. I've got to go and see her.' Tiffany was on her feet. Peter grabbed at her arm. 'Hold on. What's going on?'

'Peter, let go of my arm,' she seethed quietly through clenched teeth.

'Sit down a minute and calm down. What's going on?'

'Look, Grace has . . .' Tiffany had to bite her lip and stop talking otherwise she knew she would cry.

'I know, I know,' he comforted. 'It seems as if Grace has been stirring it between us, but she didn't succeed, did she? We're here, back together. Maybe she just didn't think that I was right for you.'

'Oh, Peter.'

'What? What is it?'

'It's much deeper than that. She's trying to destroy my life.' Tiffany stopped to blow her nose with the table napkin; she couldn't stop the tears spilling from her eyes.

'That sounds pretty extreme.'

'Oh, yeah?' Tiffany explained to Peter how she had discovered what Grace was up to by going to the school and stealing her sister's post.

'So what are you going to do?' Peter asked with great concern.

'I have to go there. I have to. I mean, what else has she done? What other things are going to come to light? If we hadn't got back together I would never have known what she said to you. I have to talk to her. I have to find out why she's doing all of this. What has she got planned with Perry? Why is he going to stay with her?'

'You've got a right to know, but will she tell you? She's obviously not all there. In light of what she's done, you know that much for a fact.'

'I've got to go, Peter. I'm sorry.'

'I'm coming with you. I don't trust her.'

As they left the restaurant, the waiter came out of the kitchen with their starter.

'I think that we do quite a fast service myself,' he thought huffily, as he looked at their empty seats.

38

Brixton, 24 July 1985

It was only when they had arrived and were waiting outside in her car that Tiffany questioned whether their visit could be dangerous. They were about to face a woman who, to say the very least, didn't think much of her and was possibly mentally disturbed to boot, and a man who may have once loved her but whose feelings for her now might be closer to hate. Well, whatever would be, would be. She wasn't about to walk away, but this was her fight, her argument. Whatever she was going to face, she wanted to do it alone. This wasn't about Peter.

'Peter?'

'Are you ready to go in now? We've been sitting here for ages.'

'No. It's not that. Listen, I've really got to do this alone.'

'Don't be silly. I'm here for you. I can't let you go up there on your own.'

'But what if she reacted in the way she did because of you?'

'What do you mean? Shit, how can anyone hear anything

around here? It's as though everyone's in competition with each other as to who can play their stereo the loudest.'

'Look, you said it yourself. What if all of this was because she was jealous of my relationship with you? She might have fancied you herself or something and, knowing that we were together, maybe that made her react the way she did?'

'Tiffany, I don't think that . . .'

'And I don't know how Perry is going to react to you. I have to go in there on my own, Peter.'

'I really would feel better if . . .'

'Peter. I know both of them. I know what I'm doing.'

It was now eight-fifty. Being a model had taught Tiffany about punctuality. If you were ever late you had to pay a fee to whoever you kept waiting and this soon made you respect time. She hoped that Perry hadn't fallen prey to that well-known illness, B M T (Black Man's Time). His letter said that he would be there at nine. If he was late today it wouldn't do her nerves any good, and Perry used to be . . . Well, it made no sense thinking about what Perry used to be; what was Perry going to be like *now*? She hadn't seen him for nearly two years. Would he have changed? Would he still have his good looks? Would he have lost even more weight than when she last saw him at Lowestoft? She wondered what their first words would be. She had to wait for him to arrive before she went up.

She sat there in silence with Peter, looking up at the windows of Flat Seventeen where lights were being turned on and off as Grace moved from room to room.

By ten-twenty there was still no sign of Perry and Tiffany began to worry that maybe he'd sent a letter after the one she had read, saying that he was going to arrive earlier. He could already be in there. Oh boy, that was something new to consider. But if he was late . . . well, she could describe him to Peter and he could toot the car horn as a warning to her if he showed up after she went in. Oh, bullshit. She'd never hear it above all this racket anyway. This wasn't a scene from a film. Either way she had nothing to lose. She was going in.

39

Ealing,
24 July 1985

Perry couldn't understand it. Where could she be, out so late with Chantelle? Had she seen him coming and decided not to open the door? He doubted it, but this was his fourth visit that night. Maybe Grace wasn't totally up to date? Maybe Tiffany was out with yet another man?

Marcia nearly tripped over him as she walked along the balcony of the council block towards Tiffany's flat.

'I take it that Tiffany's not home, then? Who are you?'

'Who are *you*?'

'A friend of Tiffany's.'

'Well, friend, tell her that Perry was here, and I'll be back!' With that he hurled his bag over his shoulder and headed for the lift.

'Charm personified,' Marcia said sarcastically. 'So that's the famous Perry. And a further element, no doubt, of a brilliant story.' Marcia waited for him to leave before using a key to enter Tiffany's flat. She'd had to drive all the way back from Islington because she'd forgotten Chantelle's school uniform. She smiled to herself. She'd had to leave Patrick babysitting and he hadn't liked that idea at all.

40

Brixton,
24 July 1985

Tiffany's foot stopped the door from slamming in her face
and kicked it back at her sister.

'What the fuck do you want?' Grace reeled from the
force of the door coming back at her but she didn't let go
of the bottle of Scotch in her hand. Tiffany could smell
the alcohol on her breath.

'Perry! Are you in here?' Tiffany pushed past Grace
and made a quick search of the flat.

'Is he here?'

'Is who here?' Grace's voice was slurred.

'Perry. I know he's coming. Is he here?'

'Does it look like he's fucking well here?'

Tiffany looked around her. On the day when she
took the letters she hadn't ventured further than the
front doormat in her eagerness to get away before Grace
returned. No wonder Grace had taken refuge with her for
so long. This place was a miserable dump. Compared to
this, her flat was Buckingham Palace.

'Well then, I'll wait.'

'Not in here you won't.'

'What's your problem? What the hell is your problem?'

'Piss off!'

'No, I want an answer. What is wrong with you?'

'Don't you get it yet, fool? *You're* my problem.'

'I'm your problem? All my life you've treated me like shit. But what have I *ever* done to you?'

'Just get out of here.' Grace threw her fist in the direction of the door. 'I don't want to know.'

'Tell me why. What have I ever done to you?'

'I said get out. Do you hear me?'

Tiffany ignored her. She needed to know. She'd let it fester for long enough and now she wanted answers.

'I've thought about it so much and I don't understand. I've never done anything to you. *Never*!'

'Are you fucking deaf?'

'I've never done anything to you!' Tiffany repeated.

'Right!' Grace clapped her hands in mock congratulation. 'Finally. That's about the only thing that you've got right. That's absolutely right. You never, ever did anything, did you, yet ...' Grace began to shake her head in disbelief '... yet why is it that you always get everything? You were Mum and Dad's favourite, you stole Uncle Kema's heart, you just have to walk into a room and people look at you in a completely different way to the way they stare at me. You've never had to try to do anything!'

'That's not true. It's not true and you know it. I ...'

'No, I don't know any fucking thing but this. It's hard to be like me. Do you know that? Do you know what it's like to be like me? Well, I'll tell you: it's hard, right. It's so fucking hard. I've had to work for EVERYTHING.'

'So have I.'

'Yeah, in a horizontal position. Just wiggle your arse, wink your eye or show a bit of leg and they all come running, don't they? It's your own fault Kevin raped you. He didn't really fancy you. It was just because you were pretty, that's all. You make me feel sick. *D'you hear me?* Sick!' Grace left Tiffany standing there as she walked into the kitchen. She was going to get a knife. If she waved it around, her stupid sister would get the message that she didn't want her there.

'You're mad. How can any woman be blamed for a man raping her?'

'Woman! You weren't a woman then. I don't even know if you're one now.' She looked at Tiffany distastefully from head to toe. 'It had nothing to do with being a woman. You had a pretty face, that's all.'

'You're just talking about the way I look, but I didn't make myself. How is it my fault?'

'You see, you do NOTHING and get EVERYTHING. SEE? Do you know that I can't have children? Did I ever tell you that little bit of information? And there you are with a child and you don't even know how to look after her, you don't pay her any attention, you put your men before her; you don't deserve to be a mother.'

'What are you talking about? It was you who tried to take over my role. I *do* pay my daughter attention. All the time.'

'Really?'

'Yes, really. It was you who wished Chantelle harm. Look at what you wanted to do to her.'

'If you really cared and took an interest, how come you've only just found out about her school?'

'Because you went to great pains to try to hide it from me, that's why, you weirdo.'

Grace looked at her and didn't like what she saw. Her baby sister, immaculately dressed, her baby sister the mother, her baby sister the model, her fucking baby sister. It drove her mad. She didn't want to see her baby sister any more. Since childhood she'd had to endure her and now she just had to get rid of her. She had to get her out of her life.

'And I've worked hard, too. Do you think that it was easy for me . . . ?' Tiffany jerked her hand up as a shield but the bottle smashed into her face. 'Oh my God! Are you crazy!' she screamed, holding her hand up to her face and realising in fear that she was covered in warm, wet blood. She tried to make a run for it. Grace grabbed her.

'I gave you a chance. I told you to go. I told you to get out, but no. You didn't listen. You must listen to me,' she screeched, shaking Tiffany. 'Don't you know that yet?'

She raised her hand and plunged the knife down, catching Tiffany's shoulder. Tiffany froze in shock, staring at the blood on her blouse. For the first time she understood her life was in danger and she automatically retaliated in a frenzy of self-defence.

Panting heavily, she hurled her body at Grace, grabbing at the knife. Grace kept twisting it from right to left, right to left, slicing the palms of her hand. The volume of flowing blood prevented Tiffany from getting a firm grip on the knife, and each time her hand slipped she received yet another cut. She had to make Grace let go . . .

'. . . or I was sure that I was going to die,' she recalled. 'I went for her eyes and Grace cried out but she let go of the knife, so I didn't waste any time, I grabbed it and I don't know how many, ten or even twenty times, I really don't know, but I stabbed her body. I stabbed her for every single wicked thing she did to me. Oh, Peter,' she appealed, 'what have I done?'

'What *have* you done? Hold on. Just wait there!' He raced into the building leaving Tiffany leaning weakly against the car, holding her head. Her hands were covered in blood.

When he arrived at Grace's flat Peter slowed down. He couldn't possibly have prepared himself for what he saw. The arms flopped loosely on either side of the body sprawled on the floor. There seemed to be pieces missing from it.

And the blood was everywhere – on the carpets and splashed around the surrounding walls. On the floor lay a knife with a long, blood-stained blade.

Peter ran back to Tiffany. He might be in a state of total frenzy but he still had the presence of mind to look around, worrying that someone might recognise him. Did she realise what she had done? They were only supposed to be going out to dinner that night. What the hell was he supposed to do now? She'd ruined everything. Peter Duvall involved in a murder? Shit! How could he have got involved in this? OK What to do? He had to think. Think!

Then he remembered their conversation earlier that day, his commitment of undying love. He couldn't abandon her now. He loved her. He had to protect her. You had to stick by the one you loved when times were hard. But then he reminded himself of what it would do to his career to be involved in a scandal like this. He remembered the flack hurled at a friend of his just for being an acquaintance of a known murderer, much less the murderer's lover – or even prospective husband. Christ! It wasn't what he should have been thinking about right now, but he couldn't help it. He knew full well what the tabloids would do with this and, undoubtedly, his career *would* suffer as a result.

He found Tiffany where he'd left her, leaning against her car door. Only then did he notice that the car was parked under the direct glare of a street lamp. The first thing that he had to do was get away from there before anyone saw them. He opened the passenger door and pushed Tiffany inside. Speed was of the essence and she was acting as though she was in a daze. He roared away in Tiffany's Mercedes at high speed, leaving the sounds of soul and reggae roaring in the streets behind them.

They said nothing on the journey back to his mansion in Kent. When they arrived he told her to take off all her clothes and have a bath. She obeyed while he burned her clothes in a heap in the grounds behind the house. He watched the flames rise high and spit out almost in fury. He used the time away from Tiffany to work out what he was going to say to her. She'd told him how it happened but, still, how could she have lost control like that? He needed time to talk to his lawyer. Could it be the case that even in driving Tiffany away he had already committed a crime? He flung her shoes into the flames and went to call Michael. He needed some advice.

'You what?!' Michael bellowed. There was the sound of a dinner party going on in the background. 'Hold on. Let me take this upstairs.'

'You have to go to the police, now. D'you hear me? Now!'

'I have to speak to her first. I have to tell her what I'm going to do. See what she wants to happen.'

'Why? She's committed a murder. What follows next isn't up to her. Call the police now!'

'I knew exactly what you'd say but I just needed to hear you say it. As I was burning her clothes . . .'

'You did *what*?'

'I told her to take her clothes off and I burned them. I wasn't thinking. I don't want to get involved any further. I thought that was the best way to handle things.'

'Listen to me, Peter. You are involved and you could be in serious shit here. At the very least you've attempted to pervert the course of justice. I'm on my way round.'

'Who was on the phone?' She emerged from the passageway nervously, wearing a white towelling bathrobe, rubbing her hair with a towel.

'Tiffany, we've got to call the police.'

She was surprised at his reaction. Hadn't he had time to think? Couldn't he see how they could get away with this?

'No we don't. I was thinking while I was in the bath.'

Tiffany kneeled down by his side and stopped drying her hair. No-one had seen them there, had they? No-one knew that she was going there? No-one even knew that Grace was back in contact with her again except Chantelle's school.

'Peter, it won't be linked to me.'

'Tiffany, it will.' Peter opened up her hands. 'Look at your palms. How are you going to explain that away? And your shoulder.' A red circular patch was already forming on the white robe. 'You're going to have to get that seen to. God, this whole thing is like a nightmare! You can't hide this. Your blood will be all over the place; all over her flat!'

'But they've got to match it up to mine before they can say that it's mine. They won't link it to me. They won't even know that we're related.'

'Has the shock made you take leave of your senses? The police aren't stupid, you know.'

'I know that but . . .'

'But nothing.'

'Look, it shouldn't be up to you. Why are you making the decisions about what should happen?'

'Because I'm involved. I drove you away. It might seem as though I colluded with you to hide the evidence by burning your clothes. I just panicked. I didn't realise what I was doing. I should have driven you straight to a police station.'

'Didn't you do what you did because you care? You wanted to protect me. I mean, think about what you said. You drive me to a police station and then what?'

'And then you tell them that you killed her in self-defence. You tell them that if you hadn't defended yourself she would have killed you, that's all.'

'And then what?'

'And then nothing.'

'Oh yeah, right. Oh, we're sorry that you and your sister had a tiff, excuse the pun, which ended in your sister losing her life. Never mind, but thanks for telling us. Have a nice day ... Sure, that's really going to happen. They'll lock me up!'

'Look, my lawyer says you've got no choice.'

'You spoke to your lawyer? Oh, so that's who you called.'

Tiffany stood up and walked over to the mantelpiece. 'Did you call him to see how he could help me, or how he could help you?'

Peter didn't reply.

'Oh, I see. Well ... your love didn't last very long, did it?'

'What has love got to do with it?'

She looked directly at him. If he had to ask her what love had to do with it then he really didn't love her in the first place. When things are down for him everyone has to jump, everyone has to rally round. He'd called her in the dead of night when he needed her and she'd dropped everything just to be with him, but now that the tables were turned ... She needed to get something straight. She needed to make something very clear before she jumped to the wrong conclusion.

'Look, as far as I'm concerned you're not involved in this at all. If anything comes out, I got in my car and drove over here or ... actually, that's it. I don't even have to be here. No, I didn't drive here. I'll leave now and, as far as you're concerned, you don't know anything about anything, right?'

'Tiffany, I ...'

'Just leave it, Peter. You don't have to say anything. I don't think it will be linked to me, much less you. I'm not going to tell them that you were there, or that you were involved.'

'But I wasn't. Tiffany, there's no other way out of this. We've got to call the police.'

'But think of the pub ... Oh, that's it. You're already thinking that the publicity will hurt your career, right?'

'I can't deny that ...'

'You really are a selfish bastard!'

'*I'm* a selfish bastard? Look, we're not talking about theft or even adultery! You can't just sweep what you've done under the carpet. What are you? Crazy? I told you in the restaurant that Grace was crazy. Now I can see that it runs in the family!'

Tiffany stared at him and for the first time saw him in a completely different light. He should have been helping her come to terms with what had happened, not thinking of the best way to deal with it to save his career.

'Forget the selfish part. You're just a bastard! No wonder your wife committed suicide,' Tiffany screamed as she ran out of the room, throwing the wet towel in his lap.

She jumped into her car and headed for home.

41

London,
1985

As she drove, her shoulder began to throb. She hoped that it was a superficial wound. She'd heard about them in films. With such wounds the victim was still able to function properly. They didn't die or anything. In most cases the bullet had just scraped the surface of the skin. But every time she had to steer to the left or the right she could feel even more blood oozing out. She looked at her shoulder. The white towelling dressing gown was bright red and the patch was growing.

A feeling of nausea welled up in her stomach and dizziness engulfed her. She had to pull over. More importantly, she had to get help. But who could she turn to? The only person who knew anything about this was Peter and he had clearly showed what his intentions were. She'd left in a hurry, in a state of fury; maybe now he would have had time to reflect, to think about the results of any actions that he had decided to take. He couldn't possibly shop her.

She saw two empty phoneboxes side by side and pulled over. She realised that she had no money, but it didn't matter, she would reverse the charges.

'Operator, can you put me through to Hazelhurst 44378?'

'It will cost fifty pence for me to connect you.'

'No, can you reverse the charges?'

The operator dialled the number and she could hear Peter's voice as he answered the phone.

'I have a call for you from a London payphone. Will you accept the charges?'

'Who is it?'

'Caller, what is your name?'

'It's Tiffany. Can you hear me, Peter?'

'He can't hear you. The connection is only one way, so that you can hear him.' The operator went back to Peter. 'Her name is Tiffany.'

'Michael, it's her again.' There was a long muffled silence while Peter covered the receiver and had a conversation with his lawyer. 'No. I won't accept the charges.'

'You bastard!' Tiffany hurled.

The operator cut her off. It was twelve-thirty in the morning.

Tiffany sank to the bottom of the phone booth, holding the receiver to her stomach. The nausea was rising again. She vomited all over the dressing gown: even though she hadn't eaten that evening, what she expelled was green in colour and very bitter.

'God! Please help me. I need help,' she begged.

How could this have happened to her? She didn't understand what was going on. And why was she bothering to ask God for help now? She had done it so many times before throughout her life and how had he responded? He'd taken away her parents, given her a demented sister, who she had just . . . Was life worth living? She had to believe that it was. She had to believe it at least for Chantelle's sake. Oh, Chantelle. What have I done to you?

Tiffany had to try to think clearly and logically about her next move, but she couldn't. She was in too much pain. She felt so depressed. There was only one thing left for her to do. She dialled for the operator.

'Tiffany, do you know what the time is? It's one o'clock in the bloody morning. Where are you?'

Marcia could hear Tiffany crying, but she wasn't responding to any of her questions. 'What's happened? Tiffany, where are you?'

'I don't know,' Tiffany managed. 'I need help. Can you pick me up?'

'What's going on? What's happened?' Marcia insisted. 'Look, if you want me to pick you up, you have to tell me where you are.'

'I don't know.'

'Find out!' Marcia screamed.

Tiffany tried to pull herself up using the cord of the telephone. The slightest movement was causing excruciating pain. As she stood, she was able to read the location of the phonebox she was in.

It took Marcia over an hour to reach her, and at first she thought that Tiffany must have left. There was no sign of her in the phonebox but when Marcia opened the door, Tiffany fell out. She tried to link her arm around Marcia's neck. Marcia thought at first that she was drunk and cursed her for not knowing when enough was enough.

'Where's Peter? And what's that stinking smell?'

Tiffany didn't speak. She felt so weak and needed some sleep. 'Can you just take me home? I'm so tired.'

Marcia pulled her Fiesta over on the road as she arrived at Tiffany's flat. The blue lights on two police cars parked outside were flashing as the sirens revolved with the sound turned off. And she could just make out two police officers standing guard outside Tiffany's door. What on earth was going on? Maybe Perry had tried to break in and had been caught? She didn't know what was happening but she wasn't going to hand Tiffany over to anyone until she found out herself. She'd been nanny to her clingy child, picking her up from school and constantly looking after her, she'd been woken up in the middle of the night on several occasions by Tiffany and now it was pay-back time. She wasn't doing all this for the good of her health!

Her journalistic instinct had smelled something big and that was the only reason she had hung around, so there was no way that she was going to miss out on this! She drove on past and decided that Tiffany would have to stay with her until she found out exactly what was going on.

'I've got a feeling that you're going to make me a million,' she told Tiffany, who was fast asleep across the back seat of her car.

She left Tiffany in the car and went to get Patrick out of bed. He wouldn't be at all happy, he'd already had to share the evening with Tiffany's daughter. If she could she'd have left him right out of it, but even though she lived on the ground floor she needed help to lift Tiffany out of the car.

'I've never seen her like this before.'

'No, nor have I.' They steadied Tiffany, took an arm each and led her into the flat. As they placed her on the settee Marcia went to shut the door to the bedroom where Chantelle was sleeping.

'Marcia, what did you say had happened to her?'

'She's drunk, that's all.'

Patrick looked down at Tiffany as she lay in the blood-stained bathrobe. Her hands were clasped tightly as if they were glued together. He gently prised them apart. They were full of flakes of dried blood.

'Marcia! I think that you had better have a look at this.'

All they could do was speculate. Had Peter done this to her? Was that why the police cars were outside her flat? Did Perry have anything to do with it? They could ask all the questions they wanted, but as long as Tiffany lay asleep they remained unanswered. They'd have to wait until she woke. Marcia took off the robe, wrapped her shoulder with a long piece of cloth and put her into their bed.

Patrick slept on the settee, Marcia sat opposite him in an armchair and worried about how she could get Chantelle off to school with Patrick in the morning as soon as possible. It was important to get her out of the way quickly: Tiffany wouldn't talk if she was around.

Marcia and Patrick woke early, washed and dressed and then Marcia got Chantelle ready, giving her breakfast in the kitchen.

'Are you going to wait for her to wake up or are you going to wake her?' asked Patrick. 'Do you want me to take a day off?'

'No, you go to work. Actually I need you to take Chantelle to school. Can you do that for me?'

'Sure.'

'If I need you I can always call, can't I?' Marcia opened the bedroom door and peered in to see if Tiffany had stirred. 'I think I should let her get as much sleep as possible, don't you?'

'Yeah. What do you think happened? Those cuts on her hand and that chunk missing from her shoulder? Yuk! You'll have to take her to hospital. How will you manage?'

'I might have to call an ambulance. I'll see how much strength she has when she wakes up.'

'Are you sure you don't want me to stay? I can get another teacher to cover my first lesson.'

'I'll be OK. Really. Just take Chantelle and I'll call you.'

He might not have agreed with her tactics or motives for questioning Tiffany, so it was best that he wasn't around. As soon as he left, Marcia ran for her tape recorder. She had work to do.

It wasn't until eleven that Tiffany stumbled out of the

bedroom. Marcia was in a chair, busily scribbling in a note pad, and she jumped when Tiffany spoke.

'I don't know what to do. I can't go to the police.'

Marcia leapt up and guided Tiffany to the settee with an arm around her waist.

'Lie down. Do you want a cup of tea . . . or coffee?'

'No, I'm fine. You know, I've been awake for a long time, just lying there . . . thinking.'

'Are you OK?'

'I'm OK.'

'Listen, the first thing I have to tell you is that when I went to your flat yesterday evening to pick up some things for Chantelle . . .' Marcia paused to give her next words more impact '. . . I met Perry. He's out, Tiffany, and he's looking for you.'

Marcia was still fishing. Did this have anything to do with him? She waited for a reaction but got nothing. Tiffany was well aware of the date of Perry's release. She had expected to meet him last night. So while she was waiting for him in Brixton, he'd been looking for her in Ealing. Great!

Marcia continued.

'You have to talk now. You have to level with me. I mean, have you seen your shoulder – your hands?' Tiffany didn't answer. 'I need to know what happened to you yesterday.'

'Oh, Marcia, it goes back much further than yesterday.'

Tiffany stretched out her legs and crossed her feet over the arm rest. She slowly bent her elbow over her face, the throbbing pain in her shoulder increasing. 'I didn't think it would be a good idea to look at my shoulder. I assume that you put all of this on it.' She looked at the material around it and covered her face again. 'I figured that if I moved it it might start to bleed again. It's bloody painful, too, and besides, I started to feel giddy just looking at my hands.'

'It's very deep, Tiffany. Really, you've got to go to a hospital.'

'I can't do that. If I go to a hospital they'll want to know what happened. If they find out, well, that will be it.'

'You know that Patrick's mum's a nurse, so let me warn you, if you don't go now, it will turn to gangrene. You'll have to go soon but do you want to talk first?'

Marcia's finger was poised over the record button on her hidden tape recorder. Patrick's mum was a nurse and had told her a lot of horror stories about injuries that she'd dealt with at the hospital where she worked. She felt duty bound to warn Tiffany of the possible consequences of delaying medical treatment, but she could also see that Tiffany needed to talk and that suited Marcia fine.

'I want to talk. I can talk about it now. I have to talk to someone.'

There was a long silence, maybe ten or fifteen minutes, before she began.

'I've been trying to work out exactly when it started but I'm not quite sure really. I think that it must have begun when I was born and Grace was five. My mum always told me that she used to steal the dummy out of my mouth and pinch me for no reason ...' Tiffany related what she thought was the whole story, spanning everything from her childhood, the fatal car crash that had taken her parents away, the home, the rape, Grace's comeback, Perry, Chantelle, her career, Peter – everything that had happened right up to and including the events at Grace's flat yesterday. While she spoke her words were recorded and as tape after tape was filled without Tiffany's knowledge, they were replaced by new ones.

Tiffany looked up at the clock. It was now two in the afternoon.

'Is it OK to have a bath?'

'Of course it is. I'll run it for you.'

'No, I'm all right. I can do it. If I have a bath now, I'll

be in time to pick Chantelle up. In all of this shit I forgot that I had promised to take her to the Pizza Hut yesterday. What's so ironic is that if I hadn't put Peter before her, I wouldn't be in this mess now.'

As Marcia reflected on the amazing story she had just captured on tape she could hear the sound of a cash register ringing up mega amounts of money, and it was all hers. But it wasn't over yet, was it? There was no way that Tiffany would be able to get away with murdering her sister, no way. Did Tiffany really think that that was possible?

Marcia knew what she had to do, but she wasn't doing it for Tiffany's sake. It would just make a much better story if she was apprehended and, besides, if the police caught her sooner rather than later she would also be able to get that shoulder of hers seen to. All Marcia was doing was acting like a good citizen in reporting her. Tiffany's arrest was inevitable, so why not bring that time forward a little?

She'd got all that she wanted now, the whole story. All her life she'd been waiting for a break like this. She definitely had enough for a book and when she finished writing it it would put her in a different league, way up there. Peter Duvall would go down for this; at the very least he would be ruined. He may have brought his lawyer in, thinking that would cover his corrupt skin, but there was no way that he could wriggle out of this. That would teach him to fuck with Marcia Abiola.

As for Chantelle, when Tiffany was arrested she'd most probably go into a home, but since Tiffany was hardly ever around to look after her what did that really matter? No, it was her duty to do what was right. That was how she justified her actions as she lifted the receiver and dialled 999.

There was only one way to deal with life – look it right in the eye and say: What a bitch!